Beautiful Delusions

An Introductory Novella to Maddison's Backlist

Maddison Cole

Dirty Talk Publishing LTD

Contents

My lovely reader, I must confess.

Beautiful Delusions was supposed to be a mini freebie. A small sample of my writing, an example of the characters you can expect to find in my other works. Twelve thousand words, max.

Yet here we are, sitting at thirty-two thousand and I still feel the need to apologise. I couldn't halt Sophia's story. I couldn't pull back from the Thorn brothers once they took hold of my mind, and I feel cheated by not giving them a full length story. Yes, there's a happy ending.

Yes, there's a ridiculous amount of dick. The bullies, the piercings, the veins – you don't even need to ask. But when you reach the end of this story, when you lie in bed rocking back-and-forth tonight, pining for oh so much more...know I am right there with you.

And as a vow, know that I will bring you those delicious bonus chapters you crave in future newsletters. I will release extra dirty scenes in my Ream subscription, and there will be more of Sophia in your future. Oh that note, fully charge your clit wand and get down to the nitty gritty.

Trigger Warning:

This is a Why Choose short romance, meaning the female lead will have three love interests and refuse to pick only one. Dark themes such as schizophrenia, medication, depression and such are included. Expect excessive amounts of steam, violence and cursing throughout. Tropes include enemies-to-lovers, high school bullies, forced proximity, power plays and multiple partner sex scenes.

Dedication

For every bookworm who reads to escape.

For everyone who dreams to survive.

Chapter ONE

Do you believe in déjà vu? How about the pre-emptive feeling something bad is about to happen? That's what I've had since the moment I opened my eyes. Staring at the ceiling, I search inside myself, looking for the will to move. All it would take is one easy slide for my legs to slip out from beneath the covers, my feet to hit the carpeted floor. But it's what comes after which has me seized in place, rigged on my back.

"Ya could make a living lying on ya back Sophia," a pink blob says from the bedside table, puffing on a cigar. Smoke drifts to me, as thick as his Scottish accent. *"Least then ya won't have to make an ass of ya'self*

at this new fancy school. Not like the last one." I shudder, batting my hand in his general direction. The gummy bear quickly dissipates. I'd fallen asleep listening to an audiobook in which he runs riot around the female character's mind. Seems now I'm in distress, he's come to haunt me too.

"*Angus really isn't so bad once you get used to him,*" said-female character's voice slips through my groan. Candy Crystal, in all her fierce glory, coming to my aid. "*At least, not at first. Once he's comfortable though, you'll find him with chubby dick in hand more often than not and jelly worm spunk all over the place.*" Okay fine, I'm getting up.

Strolling directly through the fuchsia-haired mirage leaning against my new dorm dresser, I fumble about in the dark for the bathroom light. It had been late when I arrived last night, my roommate already fallen asleep as I'd paced around outside with my headphones on, delaying the inevitable. This is my last chance to complete my masters, the last school which would accept my colorful record.

Locating the light and my make-up bag, I scramble for pill bottles. Klonopin for anxiety, clozapine for the rest. Any will do. Anything to calm the nerves, the voices. To clear my brain of the hallucinations which will plague me otherwise. Closing my hand around the first bottle, I give an instinctual shake. *Empty.* The next one, *empty.* Upending the bag into the basin, my brows furrow, a sinking feeling in the pit of my chest growing. Every single bottle is light and hollow. *No.* That can't be right; I had fresh refills only the day before yesterday.

"*I wonder how much your antipsychotics would fetch on the black market,*" that same feminine voice chuckles. I spin with a glower. Pink ruffled hair shimmers in the LEDs, black leather cinching her body in all the right places. Illustrated caricatures with a watercolor edge are set into her highly statured skin, only in the way an artist's stylis could achieve. I continue to stare, expecting her to flitter away from existence. Instead, she chews and pops a large bubble of gum, the sound loud enough in my ears to make me flinch.

"Wait, what did you say?" my mind relays her words like a phone line with bad connection. The. Black. Market. My gut plummets. My feet scrape across the tile as I drive straight through Candy, ripping my roommate's covers from the adjacent bed. Striking my fist onto the shadowed, lumpy outline, memory foam cushions my knuckles. I hit again and again, a shriek escaping me. I haven't even met the fucker I'm supposed to spend the rest of the semester with, and they've already *stolen* from me. My lungs squeeze, withholding my last breath hostage.

"It's fine," I wheeze, attempting to reassure myself. Collapsing on the bed, my legs automatically curl into a fetal position. "It's totally fine. I'll attend the registration meeting, avoid people at all costs and grab some more meds after classes. Just a couple of hours," I clench the covers in my fist, rocking gently. My biceps tremble until my diaphragm finally burns enough to release the air in a gust of relief. "Just a couple of hours."

"*You know as well as I do,*" Candy murmurs, "*the pharmacist won't replace your prescription so soon. Even if you didn't have to rely on the insurance, you're utterly fucked. And not in the good sense.*" I tune her out, endless rage simmering so close to the surface, I could hurl this bed out of the closest window, myself joining right behind. No. This was supposed to be my fresh start. No one knows me here, no one needs to know the schizophrenic wreck I truly am. And with that thought in mind, I force myself to wash, dress, shoulder my backpack and storm out of the room.

Hordes of people line the hallway, a few stares catching my eye as I push my way through, not bothering to strike up any conversations. As always, my blue hair falls forward to shield my face. A thick, straight curtain I hide behind, in the same pale aquamarine as my eyes. Stained carpets lead the way to a concrete stairwell, littered with so many discarded blobs of gum, even Candy scoffs beside my ear.

"*What a waste,*" she mutters. I'm too busy trying to avoid each one like a rubbery maze waiting to ensnare my white Converse. If that wasn't bad enough, I'd hazard a guess the cleaners don't attend to the worn, once-cream railing and stained walls which smell too much like vomit and urine to be anything else. Seems I opted for the front entrance upon entering last night, or I'd have never made it up to my room.

With some small stroke of luck I don't think will continue, I make it to the ground floor and out the rear fire escape without a single mark on my sneakers, short denim skirt or oversized lilac sweater. Not the best combo but I wasn't focused on fashion. Merely surviving Candy's judgmental stare.

The dorm block is a beast of brick and one of twelve, divided into male and female residences depending on which side of the main road you are on. I'd originally entered by foot on the far south side of campus, abandoned by bus and forced to trek through streams of frat houses and sororities. Or as I prefer to call them, '*entitled living for the rich and ridiculous*'. Now the morning sun dances across tiled ceilings and a central clock tower in the distance, I follow a tarmac road towards the main buildings, keeping to the grassy bank which provides no sidewalk. Headphones on, background drowned out.

I vaguely remember there's a map stuffed into the side pocket of my backpack as sports cars whizz by, asshole's shouting something incoherent from open top roofs. Setting my jaw, I opt against looking anymore like a newbie and tackle the maze of halls beyond the parking lot as if I know exactly where I'm going. I don't, but at least I found various lecture rooms by stumbling in mid-introduction, pockets of serene gardens, an outbuilding where the visiting gym-heads and scent of chlorine were too strong to not hold a swimming pool, and where I'm going to find myself hiding most of the time – the main library.

I'd almost caved, climbing the stone stairs until I saw Candy and her gummy bear sidekick waiting by the entrance, knowing smirks on their faces. I can't let them win. So instead, I removed my headphones and strode for the student center next door. Seniors smile from the front desk, surrounded by more leaflets than workspace.

"Hi, Welcome to Waversea. How can I help?" the girl asks before her male companion gets the chance. Both look too clean, too put together for this time in the morning. All brunette hair, beaming smiles and smart shirts holding name tags. Candy's voice flitters through my mind, advising me to ask where the nurse's office is. Nurse's have drugs. We like drugs.

"No," I shake my head, wrinkling up my nose. Kyra, as her nametag states, raises her brows. "I mean yes, please. I'm looking for Dean O'Sullivan's office? I have a registration meeting at..." I trail off, catching sight of the large clock beyond the reception area. One. Hour. Ago. "Dammit it," I curse under my breath.

"I'm afraid the Dean had to attend to a situation and has back-to-back meetings for the rest of the day. I presume you're Sophia Chambers? This was left for you," she removes a large brown envelope from a drawer behind the desk. It's heavy, as I imagine the weight of my previous transcripts are.

I peer inside just as Kyra begins to reel off everything I should have. Programme module, timetable, equipment requirements, a reading list I'm expected to have completed, an invite to join the student government and due to my situation, as she so kindly put it, a preloaded card for restaurants and cafes on site. As part of the agreement I signed electronically before being accepted here, I was told of the monthly allowance I would have access to under the terms of my specialist scholarship. Something I hope Kyra and no one else knows of.

Nodding my thanks, I leave on numb legs, pausing outside the electronic doors. I'm not required to start classes until tomorrow, but I wish I had the distraction now. Looking towards the library, I feel the tug. The pull of a thousand worlds ready to be unleashed on my mind, to fill my dreams with words where acceptance comes so easily. Where love truly exists. I'm halfway there without realizing when my shoe skids on the pavement, a small voice reaching my ears.

"Billions of ice and rock fragments. Billions of ice and dust. No, wait...was it..." Peering around the corner, an alcove against the student block becomes visible. Wooden in structure, a pointed roof shrouded in layers of wisteria, white as jasmine and swaying gently over the entrance. Through the gaps, I see her sitting on a bench only big enough to seat two. A timid girl with bunched shoulders. Thin, pale and wringing the strap of a handbag in her lap, chewing on her marred bottom lip. "Yes, that's it. The fragments are torn apart by Saturn's gravity. Billions of ice and rock fragments coated in dust form the rings. I think. Oh fuck, wait no-"

I step closer, intent on asking if she's okay when I hear that telltale sound. The shake of a plastic bottle, the pop of a cap. I still, my heart kicking up a beat. Using her bag as a shield, she can't hide the small blue pill in her open palm from me.

"Is that valium?!" I'm unable to hold myself back, bursting through the flowers to invade her sanctuary. She yelps, flinching as if she can also see Candy in my peripheral, swirling a pink baseball bat around. Plastering a look of concern on my face, I kneel by her knees. A stranger filled with compassion, only looking out for her wellbeing.

"Yeah right," Angus chuckles in my head. A dirty smoker's cough I need to get rid of.

"It...it's my last one, and I have a big test in twenty minutes." The girl is shaking, riddled with anxiety I know too well. The blonde in her hair has grown out, brown roots tracing her scalp to where it's tucked behind her ears. Her eyes are wide, glazed as if she might just burst into tears and her entire being would splosh in a puddle at my feet.

"I hear you. Tests can be stressful, but believe me," I shift to sit by her side, eyeing the pill in her open palm, "you're strong. You studied, right?" She nods. "Then you must believe in yourself, face your fears and prove you're worth more than your nerves allow."

My responding smile is watery, hiding my desperation. This is for her own good – maybe a little encouragement is all she needs. Fuck knows all I need is still right there, inches away with a V printed into the pill.

"Here, let me dispose of that for you. No one needs to know," I slowly raise my fingers. She sits a little straighter, tracking my movements like a rabbit about to bolt. I'm cautious, not once rushing. Not when my own hand begins to shake, an eager sweat breaking out across my brow. My pinkie grazes her wrist, jolting her into action. Her palm moves within a blink, that precious blue pill thrust into her mouth and swallowed on a whimper. I gape at her.

"She's going to run for it," Candy warns as the girl clings to her bag and does just that. Although she's not fast enough for me. Fisting her hair, my actions aren't my own as she shrieks and I hastily cover her mouth.

"You must know where to get more. Tell me," I ground out, intent on dragging her body a step back into the shadows of the building. Muttering sounds through my hand.

"There's a party," she rasps as I give her an inch to speak. "Tonight, Thorn Manor. Ask for Lucas. He...he can get you whatever you want." Releasing her, I duck back into the alcove, hiding out long after she's fled. Raking my hands through my blue hair, I pace between Candy and Angus, ignoring the approval they try to give. I wasn't supposed to be this person anymore.

Clinging to the hope she won't squeal to the nearest person who will listen, I calm my erratic breathing. In for three, out for five, until my chest unclenches. I have a whole day to fill until this party, until any hopes of getting some form of release. Snatching up my brown envelope, I root around inside for my café card and hold it like a lifeline. If I don't have drugs, I'll take the next best thing. Coffee.

Chapter TWO

"**W**hat do you mean, my card isn't valid?! I just got it," I seethe over the counter. My knuckles are white and nostrils are fully flared. Some preppy douchebag, with his polo shirt buttoned to the top, holds up a finger, placing a quick call before coming back to me.

"The cards are valid from the first day of full enrollment," he looks me up and down like I have fleas, "which for you is tomorrow." The scent of caffeine, the clang of machinery, hiss of steaming all mock me as I hold up the line. Bunching my shoulders, I scowl, silently wishing a violent case of diarrhea on this asshole before stalking away. No drugs, no fucking coffee, what's next? Slamming my hands into the glass door, my sneakers hit the ground harder than necessary. There's only one place left to go.

Once more, Candy and Angus are waiting at the top of the library steps. I should have given up and come here in the first instance. Poised within a pointed archway, framed by intricate stone carvings, I need to use my weight against the wooden door for it to creak open. This building, like the clocktower across the courtyard, must be one of the last remaining from the original campus. Slipping inside, several floors of railings meet my gaze.

Connected by winding staircases, I find myself in the center, levels bellowing out into the ground below as well as towering above. Grand chandeliers glimmer against brass railings, the tarnished color at odds with the wrinkled and cracked spines of first editions. Dust circulates the scent of aged paper. The breath is knocked from me long before someone shoves open the door, slamming into my back. Growling, I shuffle forward.

My mind is distracted as I approach the main desk, scribbling out my details on a registration form. The bookcases, the shelves. So many shelves. So many spines waiting for their stories to be revealed. This is where I feel safe. Where worlds of heartbreak and angst await. This is where I feel sane.

"Sophia," a harsh voice snaps. I whip my head back to the woman behind the desk, her plaque naming her as Head Librarian - Mrs. Russell.

"Um, did you say something?" I blink rapidly. The gray-haired woman is well past retirement age, her back hunched from the weight of carrying heavy paperbacks for the past forty-odd years. The kind who will work here until she's forced out by new management, and then volunteer until she dies. Her bones creak like the bookshelves as she snatches the pen from my hand. Geez, she's practically part of the furniture.

"I'm locking up at ten whether you're in or out. If you spill tea on a book, you pay for its replacement," her gnarled finger points to a table across the platform. It's simple, foldable on metal legs with a cloth draped over the plastic top. A singular hot water tank steams beside a random assortment of mugs, mostly chipped, an open box of teabags, jug of milk and heap of sweetener packets fulfilling the complimentary refreshments. Not coffee, but I'll take it.

Accepting my new library card, I fix a tea and lose myself amongst the shelves. Two levels down, I find what I'm looking for. Dark romance, typically in a seedy, shadowed section with a beanbag in the corner. I don't dare touch it, not without my UV light to inspect it first. Lifting out a random book, the first one I spotted with 'wrath' in the title, I settle cross-legged on the floor. Prying open the front cover, I release a heavy sigh. At last, the figures who linger on the edge of my consciousness have disappeared, my mind empty of thought as I dive in.

***

The lights go out.

I jolt, splashing cold tea over the rim of the mug, pattering the denim of my skirt. As long as it didn't stain the pages - that's all I care about. It takes a moment of reeling to realize I'm on the last third of the book in my hand, time lost to me as much as my hold on reality. It's not uncommon for me to check out completely. Not when fiction is where my heart thrives.

Blinking through purple-rimmed glasses I don't remember pulling out of my bag to don, I squint at the overhead lights. The bulbs glow faintly as they cool, fading into darkness. A few levels above, light seeps from elongated windows, spiraling the railing like a ring of everlasting sunset. A breeze drifts downward, cutting through the balmy air with a blissful caress. No wonder it was so easy to lose myself in a world so distant from this one.

Placing down the mug, I uncurl my legs from beneath me on the floor. Laying the book down, pages splayed over my thighs, I stretch in half, holding my toes to work some feeling back into my legs. Then I draw them back into a cross-seated position and I roll my neck. Candy mirrors my every movement, leaning against the opposite shelves, one brow cocked. I know what she's thinking (obviously) - I've heard it before. A uni grad student like myself should be outside, *living my life*. Well, life generally sucks and I'm happy exactly where I am. As long as it's quiet and I'm medicated....*shit*. The time. The party.

Jumping upright, panic floods my system, crippleing my jaunted movements as I drag myself up the shelves, only pausing to slip the book back in its rightful place. Then I'm down the aisle as fast as my feet will allow. I've missed it. My chance to get more meds. Fuck it.

Today was difficult enough, getting through tomorrow will be impossible. The weight of oppression crashes down on my shoulders, the blaring of a siren sounding between my ears. Pins and needles race from my toes to calves, forcing me to hobble. The skirt grazes my thighs, in direct contrast with the baggy lilac sweatshirt covering me from neck to wrists. Too hot. Too itchy against my taunt skin. I've fucking fucked it all.

Crash.

A hard body sends me flying backwards. I hit the ground, pain slicing along my back as my assailant stands firm. Unaffected. The fading sunlight above frames his broad shoulders, his jersey too baggy to reveal what's underneath. But I felt it. The solid muscle, the radiating power. I wait for him to move or speak, to offer me a hand. A mess of light hair shifts so slightly. His head tilt could merely be a trick of the shadows, but somehow I don't think so.

"Who are you?" His voice is like melted butter, too smooth to be real. I vaguely wonder if he's real, or a figment of my vivid imagination. But I feel the drag of his gaze on my bare legs, which have remained at an awkward angle and giving his heated stare full access.

"There's two ways this is going to play out," a new female voice sounds in my head. Not Candy's. She appears then, as bright as if she has her own light source, an arm draping over his shoulders. Brown hair tumbles from her ponytail across a white sports bra, her black gym shorts hanging low beneath toned abs. Red hand wraps are coiled from wrists to fingers, hiding the coating of blood splatter which has seeped beneath her nails. Aria – from the book I was just reading.

"You can fight him or fuck him. Either one will give you the release your precious drugs would have otherwise provided."

"She's right – you've missed the party anyway," Candy pitches in, stepping into my attacker's other side. He's yet to move while my mind plays out the scenario. *"Might as well use the goods at your disposal."* Candy grabs his junk roughly and as he clears his throat, I realize I was staring straight at his dick.

Clambering to my feet, I brush myself down. Three sets of eyes are on me, one real and two imaginary. I can hardly breathe, the burden in my chest overbearing. If I walk away now, head back to my dorm, I'll lie awake all night. Replaying how I wished this encounter had gone. I'm new here, no one knows me. He doesn't know my past. Only the person I present now, and first impressions are everything.

"Play with me," I drawl. Candy and Aria smile approvingly, slinking out of sight. This close up, the faintest scent of apple and an underlying musk drifts through me, like cider on a summer night.

"Excuse me?" he scoffs, folding his arms. Biceps bulge over a basketball jersey, his stance wide against the slip of light I have left. He's athletic, strong. Probably able to bench press me and retain the cocky tilt of his head while he does it. A player, no doubt, and luckily that's what I'm in the market for. Closing the gap between us, I force myself to embody the female character I was just reading about.

"We're alone, in the dark, and I'm bored." I summon confidence from deep within, trailing my fingers over his shoulder where the jersey cuts short, his skin smooth and blemish free. He might as well be a delusion. Uncrossing his arms, the sheer size of him has my heart thumping loud enough for us both to hear it. He absorbs the very air around us. Even without seeing him properly, the way he holds himself tells me what I need to know. He's freaking gorgeous, and knows it.

"I'm not into nerds," he slides my glasses off and places them on a nearby shelf. "I only came in here to restock my paper stash." Diving a hand into his pocket, he produces a wad of rolled pages, all torn roughly. A fissure cracks my heart in half but I don't let it show. He smokes, most likely weed, meaning he's a friend I want to keep close. This stubborn ball-player might just be able to see me through my final semester. Then I'm a free woman.

"Perhaps I'm not into asshole jocks, but somehow, I think we both can pretend otherwise for a little while." Brazenly, my fingers continue to travel over his biceps, along his arms. Moving with the swiftness of a cheetah, my wrists are grabbed and I'm shoved back a step against the bookcase.

"You proposition me and then have the balls to call me an asshole?" he growls. I smile encouragingly.

"I'm Sophia," I bat my lashes. His grip on my wrists tightens. Yes, I think to myself. This is the distraction I need. The release I crave.

Dropping his head, close enough for his breath to tangle with mine, for his strong jaw to brush my cheek, he pauses. Sizing me up, studying the heavy rise and fall of my chest. If only he could see my nipples through this heavy sweater, he'd understand how ready I am to be ruined. Corrupted. Defiled.

"Now you give me your name," I coax.

"Nah. You're definitely not my type." Using his grip to shove himself back and stride away, red coats my vision. Shame heats my cheeks. Holy crap - what the fuck was I thinking?! Throwing myself a stranger in the dark?! Whatever it was, it's the same thought that has my Converse appearing in my hand and tumbling away from me in a full-bodied throw. The sneaker hits him in the back of the head.

"The fuck-" his growl is cut short by a round of laughter. Shadows appear at his back. This time, they're not from my imagination.

"I believe your new friend wants your attention, Ezra," another male voice seeps from the darkness. I can't see them, can't tell how many there are, but a symphony of low chuckles grows in volume, gritty and rough like dirt being kicked up from the ground. Whatever parallel universe I'd been in, where fear and lust mingled, vanishes. My true senses return in their entirety.

"She can have my attention, if she likes," another voice sounds. Filled with mirth, not half as deep and rumbling as the last. A ball forms in my throat.

"You know what, I'm exhausted actually. I'm just gonna..." my voice trails off as I fail to find a way to say *run for my fucking life*. So instead, I just do it.

Chapter THREE

My lungs burn as much as my legs, and in my haste – I take the dirty stairwell back to my dorm. I'd almost left the main courtyard before remembering my backpack, which wasted precious time circling back to slip through the library window I'd escaped from and retrieve it.

As far as I know, I wasn't chased, wasn't seen, but I didn't hang around to find out either. Fumbling with my keys, I duck inside the room and slam the door closed. I've barely slumped against it when the sound of the shower turning on in the neighboring room thunders. It appears my roommate has returned at last, and Aria's words replay in my head.

'Fight or fuck. Either one will give you the release your precious drugs would have otherwise provided.' As it stands, sex is out of the question so that leaves me with the unquelled rage I've been suppressing all day. Whoever is in that shower, she ruined my fresh start before it even started. Stole from me before even introducing herself. That's just plain rude.

Shimmying out of my skirt, I drag on a pair of men's boxers and switch out for a cami vest. They're my preferred sleeping attire, and much easier to brawl in. Yeah, I'm going full animalistic mode. When it comes to messing with my sanity, to sending a message that my property is solely mine, violence is required. I've been waiting for a release all day – *all fucking day* – and as the pounding of water shuts off, I'm finally about to get it. Stalking across the room, the door swings at the same time my fist does. Except she's taller than I anticipated, and she happens to be... a he.

"What the fuck?!" a strangled rasp sounds, a large hand flying to the throat I just punched. I gape, struck still at the sight of him. Blue eyes, icy in their intensity, glare wildly from a face too clear-cut to be real. Sharp cheekbones accentuate the hard jawline any catalog would start a bidding war over. Water droplets from a mess of blonde hair cascade between the planes of a hard chest, down a valley of abs, halted by the towel secured at his waist. The richness of apple shower gel hits me tenfold, emphasized by the plumes of steam escaping the bathroom. It's *him*. Ezra.

"What are you doing in the women's dorms?!" I scream, shoving at his chest. Faltering back onto damp tile, Ezra's foot slips and he falls tremendously. Slamming hard on his back, exactly as I had in the library. Only instead of his towel pooling around his waist, it unfurls completely. A glint of a plump purple head winks at me, his cock half-mast. Well... wow.

"You're in the men's, you crazy bitch!" Ezra croaks, holding his throat and the back of his head. I blink around, pushing my confusion aside for now. Ezra feels around for his towel, but I act before I can think. Ramming the sole of my sneaker against his balls, I narrow my gaze.

"You stole my fucking pills!" I nudge my shoe higher, applying more pressure until he's crying out.

"Hey Ez, you left this in the-" another male opens the front door, halting at the scenario before him, "-car." The sweater in his hand is instantly forgotten.

"Kyan! Get her off me!" Kyan doesn't react, too stunned to move. Polar opposite to the male writhing beneath me, his straight hair of onyx black pitches forward into dark eyes, curious and all seeing. Although, his beauty is something else altogether.

"*That jaw was made for eating pussy,*" Aria speaks up, appearing horizontal across my bed. Candy pokes her head up from behind, apparently acting as the big spoon.

"*Hot damn,*" the pink-haired minx agrees. Forcing my gaze back to Kyan, he jerks into action and long arms reach for me. Oh well, I've come this far now. Lifting my foot ever-so-slightly, I slam my sneaker down on Ezra's balls. *Hard.* His scream turns blood-curdling. I should worry about the future of his children, but no one wants a thieving asshole for a dad anyway.

Ducking around the room, vaulting over the crumpled bed sheets and pillows I was punching this morning, Kyan takes chase. I toss back any object that comes to hand - headphones, books, a lamp - giving him a run around until the door is left unguarded. My only escape.

Angus is in the threshold, a high-vis jacket around his gummy bear body, flashing lights in hand as if he's directing a plane to land. Skidding out on a pile of discarded clothes, I lose precious time but make it to the door. One step into the hallway, the sweet taste of freedom on my tongue turns to bitter ash as a hand locks around my throat.

"What the fuck is going on in here?" a third man asks, crowding me back into the room with his body. I recognize his voice from the library. The male I didn't get to see. *I think your new friend wants your attention.* His fingers twitch, barely considering the fact I need to breathe as he takes in the carnage of my – of Ezra's – room. The man in question has finished howling but is still a squirming heap on the floor in my peripheral vision. Vision which is quickly becoming peppered with black dots.

"Jesus Christ," he mutters at the display. I swear there's a chuckle hidden within his words but I've tuned out at this point. Gripping the forearm holding me a few inches from the ground, I uselessly claw and twist his tanned skin. My hair is pushed back from my face, pearly white teeth in a surprised smirk coming into view. "Oh hey Feisty. Looks like you truly couldn't keep away," he chuckles. I crane my face to get away from him.

"How..." My voice is small, thick with the intake of precious air. The hand holding me loosens a fraction. "How many of you assholes are there?" Then, those large fingers tighten again and I'm whipped from the room in a blur of movement. My head is covered, shielded by black cotton I can only imagine is a pillowcase, my arms snatched behind my back and tied at the wrists. Multiple hands roam my body, fastening and binding me while the one at my throat doesn't budge until I'm fully incapacitated. Not a word is muttered, their movements are too fluid to have not been practiced.

Despite knowing this, despite my stomach turning to lead, I continue to fight. Struggle, resist, twist and scream until gravity fails me. My gut slams into a shoulder, my ass high in the air. I yell for help, already knowing no one will come to my aid. These guys exude too much power, the confidence with which they carry themselves remaining unchallenged.

"*Until you,*" Candy cackles in my mind. I snarl at her, jutting out my legs and earning a sharp spank to my ass.

"Cool it," that same, easy-going and jokey voice comments. "You're going to need your energy for what we have in store." And delusions help me, I start to scream even louder.

At the base of the stairs, where the night's air seeps through my clothes, my throat becomes hoarse and I relent. Relent on screaming, on arguing with the stoic presence beneath me. At the point I would have otherwise started begging, I press my lips tightly shut, resigned to being shuffled around. Into a car, across two laps and then heaved back out a few minutes later. My limbs are heavy with exhaustion, the need for this night to be over-with riding me as viscerally as the need for my medication. I haven't been this long without it in years. And by the time I'm dumped on a mattress with just enough bounce to tug on my binds twice, I'm an irritable mix of bored and seething.

"Well Feisty," that smooth voice sounds. "What are we going to do with you?" Fingers trail my thigh, toying with the edge of my boxers. Betraying goosebumps follow the path. I refuse to react beyond that. "Or perhaps the real question is, should we leave you tied up like a hog roast or give you the chance to fight back? You seem to have a flair for violence." That hand slips beneath the binds at my knees, tugging me down the bed.

"Toss her in the forest and let us hunt the bitch 'til morning," a growl I recognize as Ezra's bleeds through the pillowcase over my head.

Unadulterated rage weighs down his tone. Apparently, he didn't enjoy his recent kick to the balls.

"Hmmm," a soft mumble comes before the pillowcase is suddenly yanked from my head. I yelp, expecting the light to assault me but only a standing lamp in the corner casts a glow over the room.

Looming over my body, the man I refused to look at earlier fills my vision. Of course, he's stunning too. As if my mind conjured him from my latest read. Bright auburn hair has been pushed back, his green eyes sharp as lasers and his smirk... I try to ignore the protruding point of his incisors, and fail. He could be my every vampire fantasy, and the clenching of my thighs proves it. He licks his lips knowingly, winking playfully.

"Whatever your planning, you're on your own Lucas," Kyan interjects from across the room. *Lucas*, as in the drug dealer I was hoping to catch tonight. Maybe all is not lost after all, and I'm suddenly inclined to play along with his game. The shuffle of feet, the movement of shadow, slink around the bed, halting at Lucas' chuckle.

"Not so fast. You know the rules." Lashing out a hand, Lucas grabs my hair, dragging me into a seated position as I jerk and screech. None of it stops him from twisting aside, presenting me to his friends like a county fair pig. "We haven't had a pet in a while and it's my turn to choose. I choose this one." I freeze, his words circling my head like a motorbike on a racetrack. Even the drumming of an engine beats within my ears, the smell of burning rubber clogging my throat. *Pet*. Three sets of eyes drop to my stunned face. Oh no, no, fuck no.

"*Sounds like fun to me,*" Candy beams, appearing on a dresser beyond Kyan and Ezra's glares. Now Lucas has turned, the light catches a scar tracking the left side of his face, from brow to where the corner of his mouth tilts into a smirk. Stubble lines his tanned jaw, emerald eyes sparkling with acute clarity.

"It is indeed your turn, Lucas," Kyan sighs. "Make it count." Grimacing with disapproval, he strides from the room, leaving me to wonder who his words were for. *Make it count.* Ezra is hot on his heels, and finally I wrench my hair free of Lucas' grip. Throwing my bound legs outwards, I catch his hip in a weak kick which topples me back onto my restrained hands.

"Now, now Feisty," Lucas chuckles, untying me. "I just vouched for you. The least you could do is drop to your knees and thank me." Leaning close enough to unlatch my arms from the binds I now realize are akin to curtain ties, I spit in his face. Disgusting, I know, but necessary.

"My name is Sophia," I grunt, throwing a punch upwards into his gut and meeting solid, steel-like muscle. *Ow.* Cradling my knuckles, I roll onto my side, spotting my backpack and small suitcase beside the bed. Wait, why is all my stuff here? Following my gaze, Lucas' smirk doesn't falter as he plucks my phone from the side pocket and shoves it into his own.

"Sophia is much too pretty a name for someone as wild as you. All the more fun for breaking, I suppose." He chuckles, patting my cheek before he too leaves the room. I lie on my back, staring at the ceiling much like I did this morning, contemplating whether I should ever leave. I knew today would be a shitshow, but somehow I've survived. It's finally over, until tomorrow and whatever fresh hell awaits there. I have classes, I have a trio of bastards to avoid and-

Click. My head jerks upright. Angus is sitting on the door handle, his chubby pink legs swinging to and fro as he confirms my suspicions.

"Looks like ya locked in for the night, lassy," he puffs on his cigar. I groan, pushing the heels of my palms into my eyes. Exhaustion claws at my limbs but I know my mind won't be able to settle. Not when I'm acutely aware of the voices beyond the door, the deceiving wetness of

my panties, the masculine room I've found myself in, complete with a private bathroom. So instead of trying to find sleep, I reach into my backpack and tug out my eReader. I can already sense the walls closing in anyway, replicating the white softness of a padded cell around my vision. I might as well immerse myself fully, I reckon, as I open the next book on my to-be-read list and dive into the Afterlife Asylum filled with mutants and ghosts.

Chapter FOUR

"Rise and shine!" The clanging of a wooden spoon on a saucepan jerks me from a restless dream. I might as well not slept at all, since visions of an asylum and evil overlord plagued me all night anyway. My eReader clambers to the floor as I reach for a pillow and slam it over my head. The clanging stops, the pillow ripped away and the morning light bursting through open curtains sears my retinas. "Aww come on Feisty, I've got a present for you." I groan at that voice, wishing it was all just a vicious nightmare. Cracking an eye, Lucas is there, all well-rested boyish charm.

"Fuck off, I'm not in the mood," I scowl. He merely laughs.

"Suppose you don't want this then?" Lifting an orange pill bottle, one of my own, he rattles the two pills sitting in the bottom. I lurch upright, almost headbutting him in the face. Trying to snatch the bottle, Lucas is fast to jerk it aside, playfulness dancing in his green eyes.

"Na ah, you need to earn it." My walls shut down and suddenly, I couldn't care less if I had the pills or not. It isn't me who would suffer the consequences, but all of those around me. Besides, I'm not selling a piece of my soul for a temporary high.

"*There's no shame in selling your soul for freedom. At least you have one,*" a woman walks into my eyeline. Not a woman – a figment of my imagination in the form of a mutated queen of hell – *Mania*. Exactly as the book I was reading described, she's littered with skull tattoos on the exposed, pale skin around a black bralette. Her hair is a mixture of black and red, her face hollowed out with a crack down the center of her forehead.

"Oh perfect," I groan to myself but Lucas confuses my words for his pursuit to blackmail me.

"Get dressed, breakfast is on the table. We've got a full day ahead before you get these," he shakes the pill bottle again. The rattle lasts in my head long after he's skipped, *literally skipped*, from the room, echoing around the dullness of my senses.

Breakfast, as Lucas called it, is a feast fit for the frat house. Lucas is sitting at the top end of the table, alongside all those they deem worthy enough to join. Unsurprisingly, there is no spare seat for me.

"Right here baby," Lucas pushes back to pat his side. You've got to be kidding me.

"Go to hell," I scowl, turning for the main door. Hands grab me instantly, the scraping of chairs drowning out my screams as every minion who recently sat quietly eating now drags me towards Lucas.

I'm no match for their strength, but that doesn't stop me fighting back with Candy, Aria and Mania mentally cheering me on. My limbs flail wildly until I'm ultimately dumped on Lucas' lap. The man in questions is grinning like the Cheshire cat which appears lazing across his shoulders. Perhaps I should behave to get my pills back, especially as Chesh winks at me.

"There. That's not so bad is it?" Lucas chuckles to his comrades on either side. Ezra is glaring my way with such disdain, I can practically taste it. Kyan is silent, as if nothing exists except his bowl of fruit, yogurt and granola. Lucas pulls a similar version my way, leaving the platters of steaming freshly baked goods down the other end of the table. Seems I found myself in health central.

"Eat up, *pet*," Ezra says. I flip him off and Lucas chuckles, again, a deep vibration resonating against my lower back.

"Or don't," he leans forward to breathe into my ear. "Your insolence is the quickest way to make me rock hard." I balk, making a move to flee. The minions, who have remained stationary at Lucas' back, step forward to forcefully hold me in place. Hands pin my wrists beside Lucas' thighs, my vest and boxers being pulled in all the wrong directions. Reaching around, Lucas lifts a spoonful of what I can only describe as rabbit food towards my mouth.

"Open wide like a good girl and I might fill you with something else."

"*Promises, promises,*" Angus muses, shimmying his gummy bear jiggle around plates of pancakes and waffles. "*I think it's time you showed these laddies who they're dealing with.*" I stall, feeling the brush of Chesh's tail tickle my cheek. I'm insane, clinically undeniably in-sane.

"*The best of us are,*" Candy settles into Ezra's lap across the table, picking up a strawberry. She only pauses long enough to spit her gum across the table into Kyan's bowl, and then pops it into her mouth. At the same time, Lucas nudges a spoon against my lips. Once, twice. Persistently knocking. Candy winks, a wicked gleam in her eyes as the other characters around me still. Watching, waiting. I can hear their thoughts loud and clear. You know what, maybe I am insane, but I reckon the best protagonists are.

Opening my mouth, the spoon glides in effortlessly. Muesli and bark scrape my tongue, incredibly dry and completely tasteless.

"That's it Feisty," Lucas praises, stroking my hair. The hands at my wrists relax, and my mouth clamps down around the spoon. Game on. Jerking my chin violently, the metal is torn from his grip. I don't bother spitting it out, spinning before Lucas can pre-empt my next move. Before he can foresee the spoon handle being thrust into his eye with a move I usually reserve for blowjobs. My fingers are in his crotch next, grabbing for whatever comes to hand first. Squeezing, twisting, yanking. Lucas squeals like a pig in a butcher shop and I don't wait around to see if I've done any lasting damage.

Flanked by Mania and Aria, I wriggle through the minion's grabby hands. Chesh slithers ahead, leading the way. Angus, with a hand clamped on the cat's striped tail, is tugged along parasailing-style, a cigar puffing rings from his wide smile. The assault of my own mind blurs within the hollers of those scrambling for my lithe body, but I'm too busy ducking, skidding across the floor to where Candy is beckoning me towards the door. Sweet freedom lies beyond, a paved walkway between luscious green grass. The perfectly fixed tarmac can't be placed anywhere other than amongst the expensive manors leading into campus, where I knew a bunch of pretentious pricks must live.

Five steps from the door, my heart leaps. Three steps and a smile is spreading across my face. One step - blinding pain erupts at the back of my skull. I scream, grabbing for the hair now fisted tight in a meaty hand. Kyan glares down at me, his black eyes like a never-ending void that make it impossible to settle on where to look.

"If one of us has claimed you as their pet," he growls, tightening his grip further, "it is a privilege. You do not fight, you don't resist. You sit quietly, eat your damn breakfast, and remember your fucking manners." Using this grip on my hair, Kyan drags me back to the center of the dining room I hadn't bothered to look at much until now. Not since I arrived in the dark and spent the night staring at my eReader.

Incredibly high ceilings seem to sparkle beyond crystal chandeliers, every wall and fixture in opulent white. Too clean for a group of young men to live in, too pristine to be used for wild parties. The only colors are soft dashes of grays in the velvet curtains and throughout the furniture. The dining table itself, now I look beyond the plates, is a slab of marble in silver and slate.

Kyan holds me at the far end of the dining room, forcing me to stare at Lucas like Lord of the castle, still in his seat at the head of the table with a stupid grin on his face. "Now, say thank you to Lucas for his kindness." Kyan growls. I set my jaw, my nostrils flaring. Beyond Lucas' back, all of the characters currently plaguing me appear, wide eyed and shaking their heads. But what am I supposed to do? This isn't fiction; this is real life. One that's rapidly being flushed down the toilet so at some point, I need to admit defeat.

"Thank you, Lucas," I grit through my teeth. I'm released so fast, I stumble into the open archway, clinging to keep myself upright. When Lucas appears before me, all shit-eating grin and mock bow, I let him lead me back to my designated bedroom, feeling my resolve drain each step of the way. Fortunately, during the commotion downstairs, the rest of my bags have miraculously appeared, stacked by the foot of the bed. At least being a 'pet' doesn't dictate how I have to dress. Not a leash or pair of bunny ears in sight.

Not so fortunately, Lucas wrangles his way in as I try to shut the door in his face. Helping himself to my suitcase, he pulls out a crocheted crop top my mom forced me to pack. Something about dressing my age. I'm not a prude by any means, but if dressing my age means having my tits on full show in a dropped cleavage, small tassels lining my sternum and the roughened wool chafing my nipples all day – I think I'll pass.

Digging out booty shorts, underwear and a pair of black Converse, Lucas shoves me into the adjoining bathroom kicking and screaming. He uses his body to hold the door closed until he manages to lock it, telling me through a slip in the wood I can't leave until I'm 'suitably dressed'.

"What the fuck has my life become?" I quietly groan to the Cheshire Cat floating around the tiled room. Drifting over a jacuzzi tub, his purple stripes seem to spiral forever as he spins upwards towards a small window above the toilet. Not huge, but maybe just big enough…

"*Quite an adventure, I'd say,*" Chesh winks, disappearing from view. Well, I can't argue with that.

Chapter FIVE

"**M**iss Chambers!" a sharp voice wakes me from my day-dream. I'm not even sure where my mind went this time, but the interactive board certainly wasn't filled with examples of transgressive and innovative forms before I spaced out. Mrs. Patrick taps her nails against her desk, waiting for me to acknowledge her. *Shit.* "Are you here to better your chances of impressing me with your dissertation, or is the sound of my voice merely a vice for you to ponder your life choices?"

"I-I'm sorry, I'm here for the lecture. Please continue," I mutter, shrinking back into my chair. She looks me over, not a shred of belief in her shrewd gaze. Reaching retirement age, her wispy blonde hair is trimmed short, a cane on hand to support her when walking around the desk.

"See me after class," she nods once, going back to the textbook everyone else seems to be following. I struggle to withhold my groan, causing a few nearby to chuckle. I try my best after that to focus, to stay on track with jotting down notes, but without my meds – it's like trying to steer a sinking ship. Every time I think I'm on track, an iceberg of random thought causes me to swerve and takes too long to unscramble the words in my notepad. By then, Mrs. Patrick has moved on and I have no hope.

"Did you guys hear?" a girl from the row in front whispers to her friends. Most grunt in agreement, except one who asks, "Hear what?"

"The Thorn Brothers have chosen their new pet." The blood in my veins runs cold. Flicking to a page in the back of my notepad, I jot down 'Thorn Brothers' and any more information I reckon I'll want to come back to later.

"What?!" the brunette gasps a little too loudly. "I've applied seven times?!" Waiting for Mrs. Patrick to turn back around, the original gossiper nods.

"Last night, apparently. They haven't announced who it is yet."

"They'll probably save it for the sports rally this weekend," a girl in the middle of the row sighs.

"If she lasts that long," another snickers. "Screwing three men at once isn't as easy as it looks in the pornos. Especially when there's nothing average about the Thorn Brothers." A ball forms in my throat, unbeknownst to the brunette who giggles.

"I heard Kyan got a new piercing recently-"

"That's quite enough!" Mrs. Patrick slams her cane on the desk, making us all jolt. "Do I need to hold a full detention to re-deliver this lecture?" No one speaks. We don't dare breathe. Once more, the session continues but there's no way I can concentrate now. Pet, announcement, three at once, piercing?! My mind is reeling, breath quickening as Candy appears in the empty seat beside me.

"It's nothing you can't handle." Reaching across, her hand seems to guide my own as I scrawl in the back of my notepad, dully watching the words appear. *Brazilian wax needed.* The bell blares, rising a yelp from my throat. Bags are hastily packed, bodies moving while I sit there, too heavily to lift my limbs. Until Mrs. Patrick looks my way, curling a gnarled finger my way.

My feet fly down the steps of the lecture hall, books clutched in my arms. The closer I get, the more disapproving Mrs. Patrick's eyes grow at the clothes I borrowed from the sports hall. She should have seen how the gym-heads gaped at the outfit Lucas had originally chosen. At least they couldn't see the wings I convinced myself where sprouting from my back as I flew over campus on featherlight feet. Now, a navy skort and white polo shirt cover me well enough, my blue hair thrown up in a messy bun. At least I was able to find my glasses where Ezra left them on a library bookcase.

"Does my class seem like a joke to you?" Mrs. Patrick starts, clicking on her laptop as she speaks. "I know of your history, Miss Chambers. Your scholarship states you must successfully graduate, or you'll have to pay all of the funds back. Given your juvenile record and the possibility of being a college drop-out, I don't know who will employ you long enough to do so."

"I'm well aware." My voice is short, clipped. I know of the vicious circle I'm in. I know of the precious opportunity I have, and which the Thorn Brothers seem intent on screwing up.

"So when I accepted you into my programme this late in the year, I'd presumed you'd be most eager to absorb what I have to teach you. I'm your last chance."

"With all due respect," I lean on the desk, my words not my own. No, this is all Candy, Aria, Mania and whoever else is living in my head. "I am my own last chance. You relay lectures you've repeated for twenty odd years, but I'm the one who will be cramming in the library each night to ensure I wipe that cynical look from your face."

"How dare you-" Mrs. Patrick scowls until her stern gaze floats over my shoulder. The next moment, an arm rounds my waist. I blink up at Kyan's clenched jaw, his black eyes making no effort to meet mine. Which is good, but I can't help myself from glancing south to see if I can distinguish the piercing rumor. "Mr. Thorn. Forgive me. I-I didn't realize..." Is that fear I sense? Indeed, Mrs. Patrick's face has pinkened, her posture hunched as she fights to make herself appear smaller.

"Now you do. Sophia is with us. Ensure your tone and manner reflects as such." Stunned, my feet shuffle as I'm guided from the room. Kyan releases me to snatch the books I was given and stuffs them into my backpack, which he seemingly brought. Then he eases the straps up my arms, planting it on my back. My hand flies to the side pocket, hunting for my phone but I should have known better than to expect it to be there.

Huffing, I stare at the man standing before me in the hallway, everyone nearby giving us a wide berth. A maroon t-shirt is stretched across his firm chest, tapered jeans fitting too snuggly to not be tailored to his thick thighs.

"What did you go to juvie for?" Kyan watches me too closely, his face devoid of emotion although his tone did dip as if he was trying to be sensitive. Unfortunately, his next words revoke that notion. "You seem too... weak to have survived a place like that." I scowl, stomping my heel down on his shoe. It has no effect.

"You don't know me," I growl. Multiple grunts back me up, but I'm the only one who can hear them. Still, Kyan waits as if I might dignify him with an answer. I don't have one.

How can I explain being incarcerated was where I developed my coping mechanism. I.e. My knack for daydreaming. I mastered imagining my own friends who comforted me post-beating from the other girls, who I sat with in the yard while avoiding all others. The best way to go by unnoticed. The only way to survive without any long-term damage. Although now I rely on drugs to silence the voices in my head, I don't know if I would consider myself a survivor at all.

"You no longer need to attend classes," Kyan finally changes the subject, stepping in closer. I hold firm as our chests brush, his shower gel of cedarwood drifting through me. "Lucas has given you a free pass. If you see out the semester with us, you'll pass with multiple job offers in your lap. All for the easy price of sitting in his." He can't be serious.

"I don't want a free ride - I transferred schools to earn my way through," my eyes narrow. Again, I'm met with that stoic silence, Kyan's jaw tight and eyes dead. Shoving him a step back, I raise my fist to punch him, to get any sort of reaction, but he catches my wrist too easily. Spinning us, I'm suddenly against a wall, caged in by thick biceps.

"Maybe you should be a little less aggressive and a little more grateful. Belonging to us means you are *ours*. To enjoy, to command, to fuck," Kyan's head dips. That jaw, that devilishly taut pussy-eating jaw, scrapes my cheek and I swear I just came a little. His lips part, brushing across mine in a whisper of a touch before it's gone. "Or to discard in any way we see fit." Whipping backwards, I stumble for the second time today because of Kyan. Gathering my balance, I find him halfway down the hall where students part to let him through. Fucking asshole.

"I hate you!" I scream, much to the shock of those watching. I don't care what they think. I refuse to belong to anyone.

"Feelings mutual," Kyan calls back, holding up a peace sign. Then he's gone and the bell rings for the start of my next lecture. Fuck, late again!

Lunch rolls around two classes later and I'm about ready to pass out on the table. Nursing a coffee, I lean over it as if I'm hungover. Two days without my meds, perhaps I am hungover. My fingers shake like a sobering addict as the rim on the plastic cup graces my lips. It's vile. Like the equivalent of what caffeinated dog shit would taste like, but it was free.

Sitting in the cafeteria, I figured I shouldn't go crazy with my monthly food card on the first day. Luckily, it's not too busy and I'm able to have a full table to myself to, as Mrs. Patrick put it, question my life choices. This is supposed to be my new start, and I won't let a bunch of righteous dickwads fuck it up for me. At least, not on day one.

Pulling my notepad out, I flick to the back page, glancing over the scribbled notes I made. Below, I write 'Game Plan' as a heading and underline it twice. Then I stare at it, failing to come up with anything realistic. Murder is out, running away won't work, learning taekwondo overnight seems like a lot of effort. Glancing over to an adjacent table, I see the same girls from Mrs. Patrick's class this morning, laughing and chatting away. There's strength in numbers, and they seem to know what's going on around here much more than I do.

"I think it's time to admit, I'm going to need some friends," I sigh to myself. Suddenly, every seat at the table is filled with women of all builds and hair colors, all smiling at me sweetly. All figments of my imagination. "Real friends," I drawl to Candy sitting opposite. She's always the ringleader. The loudest and most prominent. Pushing myself up, I do something I never did in juvie. I find some temporary courage and stride over to the popular girls, sliding into a free seat at the end of their table.

"Hey all, I'm Sophia. I just started here." I wave. For a millisecond, they all spin to raise brows at me and I think I'm about to be lynched. But then they break into smiles, the volumes of their welcomes deafening. My smile wobbles. The closest, a brunette who introduces herself as Letty, asks a bunch of general questions which I answer evasively. Then she gives me a rundown of everyone's names, which I'll never be able to remember.

"So, I hear there's a sports rally this weekend?" I casually spin the conversation. Letty offers me some of her cheesy fries as everyone's faces light up.

"Oh yes! You've arrived just in time for the quarter-finals against Radley. Our basketball team here are like gods - the Thorn Brothers being the star players. Just wait until you see them," Letty winks. I hide my blush.

"Are they like... real brothers?" I divert my gaze to the fries. The table giggles once more.

"Adopted ones, yeah," a redhead across the table answers. "Their parents are extremely wealthy but they couldn't conceive themselves so they took on the boys from an orphanage. Only went for one, ended up leaving with three. Apparently they wouldn't be separated. Now they stand to inherit a fortune, including this college." I choke, needing to down the shit-stirred coffee to clear my throat.

Letty just watches me knowingly and nods. "Yep. This college has been in their family since it was built." A shudder rolls through my entire body. I need to handle myself very carefully from now on, or it won't matter how much revision I put in. I'll be out on my ass, broke and in debt regardless. What a way to start my adult life. A girl, with jet black hair cut into a sharp bob to accentuate the sharp lines of her face, leans forward with a cunning smile.

"If you want to get on the Thorn's radar, your best bet is to check out the bulletin board." She points across to a large board by the serving hatch. I already know I don't want to look, but have to. Letty tuts, rolling her eyes.

"Don't tease the poor girl. You know she doesn't stand a chance." I conceal my frown, figuring she didn't mean to sound so harsh. The bell rings, ending my short reprieve of playing catch up. The girls stand suddenly, kissing each other's cheeks goodbye and waving to me, dispersing in different directions. When the coast is mostly clear, I slink over to that bulletin board.

Around the outside are the type of flyers I'd expect, cheerleading try-outs, upcoming dances and charity events, apprenticeship opportunities. But smack bam in the center, taking president over everything else, is a poster for 'The Thorn Pet Internship.'

Are you looking for an exciting opportunity? In the market for quality personal references and various job offers upon graduating? Do you take pride in your appearance?

Enquire below to be considered for the Thorn Pet Internship programme. The successful applicant will need to live-in, obey orders and remain enthusiastic throughout the agreed term. A decent pain threshold, tolerance for exercise and high sex drive are essential.

One vacancy per semester.

"*Well shit,*" Candy leans her head on my shoulder. I feel more presences closing in, but I'm busy trying to pick my jaw up from the floor. This is a legit advertisement, with a sign up link and everything. I'd naively thought the brothers were just making it all up, seeing how far they could push me before I went feral. Testing my limits as the new girl, or trying to scare me into running for the hills on my first day. But this... This is bigger than I ever expected, and something I cannot allow myself to be a part of.

A skid of sneakers pulls me from my thoughts long enough to see the last of those rushing out of double doors, late for class. Oh yeah - I have another three lectures before I can hide in the library until closing. But even as my feet start moving, my backpack heavy on my shoulders, I already know it's pointless. I wouldn't be able to concentrate anyway, and worse - I don't want to give anymore professors the wrong idea about me on my first day. So as much as I hate to use 'Lucas' free pass,' I enter the hallway and stride in the opposite direction of where I'm supposed to be.

Exiting the main campus, I take a detour towards the dome which no doubt houses the swimming pool. Sure enough, I'm welcomed inside by a bubbly receptionist, the length of the pool glistening beyond the glass wall at her back. She tells me to take a look around so I pass through the luxurious gym and enter a sports arena.

The bouncing of a ball forces me to remain in the shadows of the bleachers. All three brothers are there, playing ball with the rest of their team. The Waversea Warriors, as all of the banners around the arena would suggest. Chewing on my lip, I lean further against the structure, pointlessly lingering. I'd only intended to make sure they were all busy while I snuck back to their house, hunting for solace, my drugs and my phone, but for some reason, I stay.

Yellow and black jerseys hang from their brawny bodies, the elongated arm holes giving glimpses of their solid chests when they twist and duck side to side. Somehow, the baggy shorts add to the allure, their calves and biceps equally rippling with muscle. Sweat beads from their brows, slicking their hair but not at all dampening the lithe way they attack the court. Surprisingly agile in Air Jordans, I soon realize it's the three of them against all others.

Kyan bounces the ball between open legs for Ezra to retrieve on the other side. His messy blond hair is pulled back into a small bun, a smile on his face I've yet to see. Dribbling along the court, Lucas is waiting lazily beneath the net, examining his nails. A shrill whistle escapes Ezra, the ball leaving his hand one last time. Lucas jolts forward with the finesse of a large cat, pouncing to catch the ball and throw it in the same jump. It swivels the hoop, dropping south to declare their victory before Lucas has even landed.

His brothers are on him in an instant, scruffing up his hair, tickling, play fighting, laughing. The display rocks the perception I had of the controlling assholes, bringing a heavy dose of uncertainty with it. Maybe I shouldn't be here, creeping around in the shadows. Within moments, the rest of the team dive on their backs and it becomes a sweaty mosh pit of fists. Okay yeah, time to go.

"You're not going to stay for the show, Feisty?!" Lucas yells over all the noise. Everyone else goes silent at my back and I freeze. "We were just about to all get naked and shower off. Wouldn't you like to spy on that also?" I shudder, causing the hairs on the back of my neck to stand on end. The open door is only a few meters away. This scenario is too similar to this morning and I'm suddenly reminded how much these boys like a good old fashioned chase. Not to mention how fast they are.

I already know what will happen if I make a run for it, like the lighting of a fuse starting a countdown. There's no way I can outrun the inevitable explosion, but my body doesn't get the memo. In the next breath, my backpack has hit the ground and I'm speeding through the gym with my arms pumping.

"*Run Sophia! You've got this!*" a whole host of females line the side of the gym, all in matching cheerleading outfits with pom poms. Candy has a horde of gummy bears around her feet in all colors of the rainbow, Mania summons wispy shadows of demons I'm forced to vault through. Behind, the basketball team take chase, yelling for those nearby to grab me. I manage to evade a series of outstretched arms, clambering over a guy on a weight bench too busy struggling against the metal bar to bother with me.

Somehow, my sneakers hit the ground and I make it out of the automatic sliding doors. Free of the air-con, the sun slams into me with such force, I'm disorientated and turn the wrong way. An open field of lush green spans towards the woods beyond, leaving me completely exposed with nowhere to hide. My only option is to run and not look back.

"*Gorgeous place for a picnic though,*" Candy appears on the ground, clinking a champagne flute with Aria. Her hands are still bound with fighting wraps, her brown hair flowing in a long ponytail. I run through the center of their picnic blanket, breaking the mirage in half. My legs protest with each step, my lungs screaming for a rest. The treeline ahead grows closer in time with the hollering behind growing louder. Tears stream from beneath my glasses, cutting a path towards the roaring in my ears. There's a reason I didn't take phys ed, and why I reserve exercise for those in the books I read.

Somehow, the shadow of the trees slips over my feet as I launch myself into the woods. Pine invades my senses, the terrain uneven and slowing my progress. Braving a look back, there's too many silhouettes breaching the forest. A scream locks in my throat as I stumble, scraping my knee on the bark-littered ground but to my credit, I'm up and moving within seconds. I need help, a distraction.

"*You rang?*" Chesh appears before me, smiling wide and floating through the air as if we're going for a leisurely stroll. I don't let up my pace, keeping my focus on the spiraling cat. His mischievous laugh drowns out the shouting of my name, the pain blossoming at my knee. Adrenaline has taken over, as has my knack to hallucinate. I follow his path, trusting somewhere in the back of my muddled mind, I must know the route. Either that, or I might happen upon a hidden cave beneath tree roots and can hide out like a hobbit.

By some miracle, civilization appears on the far side of the wood. A tarmac road, houses, vehicles for me to hitch a ride and get the fuck out of dodge. A smile dares to stretch across my wind-beaten face, my legs starting to wobble as I hurdle over a final log and throw myself across an invisible finish line.

Pausing for only a moment, my hands rest on my thighs, the breath heaving through my chest burning too hot. Blinking to clear my foggy vision, a house sits on the other side of the road. No - not a house. 'Thorn Manor'. What?! Chesh swirls before my eyes once more, winks and vanishes. Traitorous pussy!

Arms wrap around my middle, easily lifting me from my feet. Lucas, Kyan and Ezra are all there, no sign of exhaustion marring their beautiful faces. Spotting a black SUV parked in the driveaway, those chasing me from behind skid to a stop.

"Thanks for wearing her out for us fellas," Lucas chuckles. Laughter fills my ears as I'm carried towards the manor, kicking and screaming. Catching hold of the doorway, my nails dig into the wood as I promise to kill every fucker standing outside on the lawn, smirking in disbelief, before Ezra closes the door and locks me inside.

Chapter SIX

"Haven't you ever heard of consent?! Let me go, you shitbag assmuching b-" A gag ball is stuffed into my mouth and tied at the back of my head. I continue to scream through it, wrestling against the hands pinning my wrists behind my back. Lucas stands before me, his tanned skin, glistening green eyes and easy smirk at odds with the monster I believe him to be. His auburn hair flicks forward, tickling my own forehead when he leans down to stare directly into my eyes.

"If memory recalls, it was you who sought us out in the gym." His thumb traces my cheek, which hollow as I muffle through the gag.

"No need to be shy about it, Feisty. You're curious. We gave you space to adjust today, and you came straight back. So I propose a test run. Let us show you what it could be like this evening. Wake up here in the morning, and if you decide you really want to leave, we'll move you back into the dorms." I immediately cast a glance at Ezra, hanging back to watch. Lucas chuckles, sidestepping to consume my gaze once more.

"Ezra will stay here. He only uses the dorm as a secondary escape. He isn't a fan of being social all the time. But if you want it back, it's all yours." I narrow my eyes, flaring my nostrils. There's another important aspect I thought Lucas had forgotten, but he quickly adds - "And your meds will be replaced in full. Do we have a deal?"

One evening? One night, with the three of them? It's every girl's fantasy, but Letty's words from class echo around my skull. Something about being torn in half and a new piercing. I swallow thickly. The air thickens, Lucas' stare too intense as I fight against the voices in my mind. Candy is screaming at me to accept, her groin gyrating all over my vision. Surprisingly, it's Kyan who leans into my ear.

"If at any point it's obvious you want to stop, we will. We're not rapists, Sophia. We're just... curious about you too." His words are a balm to the voices, bringing a peaceful silence. I exhale harshly, the decision already made. If I were to walk out now, I'd always wonder. Forever long for a second chance. I'll give them my trust for one night, see what it is they want to do to me, but come tomorrow - I'm gone. I've been trapped too much in my life to walk into another cage.

My head slowly lowers into a nod. I didn't even hear the clink of metal before handcuffs clamp around my wrists. That feeling alone is enough to fill me with regret, my squirming infused with panic. Oblivious, Lucas retrieves a chair from across the bedroom I've been given. Ezra opens the drawer of the dresser he's been leaning against, presenting a pair of scissors. I shake my head, backing into Kyran. His body is an unmovable wall as Ezra approaches, dragging the scissors across my collar bone.

"Don't move, or I might accidently slip and repay you for kicking me in the balls." Lowering the scissors, the next time I feel the cold metal, it's slipping beneath the white polo top I borrowed from lost and found. He cuts it clean in half before turning his attention to the skort. Maneuvering the scissors through the underlying shorts without nicking my underwear takes skill, and then the scissors are passed to Kyan to cut the rest of the shirt from my shoulders.

I'm left standing in the underwear Lucas picked out for me this morning - a hot pink lace set with black threading. A jewel hangs from where the bra connects beneath my breasts. Another purchase from my mom. Ezra's icy blue eyes drink me in, slowly, thoroughly. His face doesn't shift, but the hardening length in his basketball shorts is hard to ignore.

Lucas spins the chair, signaling for me to sit on it backwards. My gaze snags on his outstretched hand, a small whimper hidden behind my gag. I've alway been a sucker for hands - and Lucas' are beautifully veined, his palm wide, fingers long and skilled. Oh sweet mother of cum-milk.

My thighs clench as I'm shuffled forward, and lowered to straddle the chair. Kyan positions me, pushing my back inwards to tilt my ass back, hanging off the end of the seat. The Converses are pulled from my feet before my ankles are also cuffed to the chair legs. His fingers trace my calves, curling around the back of my knee and slowly stroke my thigh until he reaches the thong stretched over my ass.

Click. My head shoots upright, noting the closed door before twisting to look around the empty room. Only Kyan and myself remain, aside from the audience of my delusions sitting in deck chairs passing around popcorn. I squeeze my eyes closed.

"It's okay, Sophia." Kyan breathes my name too softly. Gone is the man who rallied me against the wall and called me weak earlier. Gone is the man I could easily hate, and I kinda want him back. Anything to avoid feeling like I trust him.

"They need to shower while I prep you," Kyan continues. My heart thunders so loud, I hear it through my ears. Holy shit, this is really happening. I brave a look over my shoulder, my blue eyes large and pleading. For what, I'm not sure. Wetness soaks through my thong, the anticipation driving me crazy. Kyan lifts those endless black eyes and smooths his similarly colored hair back.

"Oh, don't look at me like that. I need you to keep hating me so I don't have to regret the handprints I'm about to leave on your ass." There he is. I scowl, a rough sound emanating from my throat. "That's better," he smirks condescendingly and delivers the first spank. I jerk, choking on my gasp. The sting fades almost instantly, not meant to hurt but to shock. From then on, I face forward and wait. And wait, until I grow twitchy. A shudder rolls through my back, my groin shifting on the edge of the seat.

Suddenly, his tongue licks the seam of the thong, clit to ass and back again. Kyan sucks the material into his mouth, humming to himself. His nose nudges at my opening as he takes his time, savoring and inhaling me. That devilish tongue spears me once and then is gone, a hard slap hitting my other ass cheek. This one is slightly harder, drawing a groan from me. My pussy is throbbing, my head hazy.

The sound of a vibrator comes just before its plump head touches my clit, on the outside of the thong. That damn scrap of material barring me from the full force of tremors. I strain against the handcuffs, clawing to shift the thong aside when Kyan withdraws fully. I scream around the ball in my mouth. Not like before, where I was fighting to get away, but a beg. A shameless plea to drive me toward the orgasm tantalizing the edge of my consciousness.

"Are you going to behave?" Kyan asks from too far away. I nod. Angus help me, I nod like a freaking bobble head, jutting my ass back further. Resting my breasts against the soft gray suede of the backrest, Kyan thankfully resumes his position. Kneeling behind me, his full attention on stroking the clit wand along the length of me. Clit to back, over and over. Just when I get used to the rhythm, rolling my hips in time, Kyan changes pace. One finger enters me, long and steady.

"Fuck, Sophia. You're so tight," he mutters. I bite down on the ball, lost to the feeling of him adding another finger. "We're in for a real treat with you." The vibrator meets my clit this time without any barriers, sending me into an inevitable spiral. Kyan pumps his fingers, twisting them on the way out. I'm so close, too close to surrendering everything I am and letting them have their way with me. Tremors prickle at my legs, my nipples aching. Thrusting in hard, Kyan keeps his fingers still, applying pressure to my g-spot as the vibrator works its magic. I tip over the edge, waves of bliss crashing through me as Kyan's teeth sink into my ass. The harder he bites, the harder I cum.

My muffled screams fill the room, signaling for the door to open. Ezra and Lucas walk in, their muscled bodies still pebbled with water droplets. Both wearing matching navy boxers, the tight kind, they prowl forward. Kyan swiftly withdraws. I whimper at the loss of contact.

"That was quick," Ezra states blandly, as if I was being tested on my endurance. I can't summon the energy to care right now, my head slumping on the backrest. Lucas, in all his humored beauty, tugs my head up by my messy bun.

"How does our pet taste?" he quirks a brow, speaking over me. Kyan, beginning to exit, stops as their shoulders bump, lifting his two fingers coated in my juices. Both keep their eyes on me as Kyan's fingers enter Lucas' mouth, his lips closing tight as he cleans my evidence from his brother's fingers. I swear, I just came again.

A third spank hits me and I see stars. Only now do I realize Kyan was going soft on me. Ezra has no such reservations. His smacks are bound to leave me red and raw, on my ass, my thighs. He hits me until Lucas barks, "That's enough." My reprieve is ruined as his fingers push into my pussy, at least three at once.

"She fucking loves it," Ezra disagrees. I can't argue. My body isn't currently my own. Only an instrument for them to pleasure and draw orgasms from. Withdrawing just as sharply, Ezra nudges rather than hits me this time. "Spread your cheeks." I obey, rotating my cuffed hands to open my ass wider. The thong is instantly cut away. I brace myself for Ezra to continue his payback, understanding his bruised ego needs to be repaired, but instead - he and Lucas switch positions.

Everywhere Ezra lashed me, Lucas' fingers stroke. Soothing away the pain, tenderly replacing them with a loving caress. I continue to hold my ass, presenting myself to his every whim. Ezra stops before me, gripping my chin in one hand and releasing the gag with the other. My jaw clicks as I stretch my mouth, licking my dry lips to regain feeling. Without releasing my chin, Ezra tugs his cock free of his boxers. It juts right in front of my face. Holy hell. He was impressive when I saw him half-hard last time, but now... he's thicker than I could have imagined.

"Bite me and I'll fucking destroy your ass," is his only instruction before shoving his cock into the back of my throat.

"*Well, now you're going to have to do it!*" Candy cries, appearing too close. I shake her out of my sight. Holding himself deep, Ezra waits to the point of asphyxiation before withdrawing. I choke, gasping for breath but he does it again too quickly. Black dots pepper my vision. I barely feel what Lucas is doing to my rear end until a lubed butt plug enters my ass. I tense, struggling to hear his soft words to relax as Ezra thrusts into my mouth. His hand has drifted to close around my throat, feeling himself enter and retract.

The men are polar opposites in their approach, but the result is the same. Even Ezra, in his forceful claiming, drives my lust higher. Like an outer-body experience, my mind reeling with sensation, they plug and fill my holes. The clit wand is replaced with another vibrator, this one gliding through my wetness but not entering me far enough. I squirm, wanting it all, if only just to prove I can take it. In the same way, I take Ezra's solid cock without complaint. It's become a game of stubbornness now, seeing how long it takes me to bow out. To admit defeat. To submit.

"Alright Lucas, kick it up a notch," Ezra growls, his voice thick. His thrusts slow as Lucas' increase, the vibrator finally hitting home. I groan around Ezra. Lucas closes his mouth around my clit, sucking, licking, nipping. Everywhere I'm being touched ignites, an inferno swirling through my core that's able to tear me apart. If only -

"My -" I manage before Ezra fills my mouth. Withdrawing slowly, he tilts his head of messy blonde hair. "My nipples. Touch them, please."

"Are you begging?" Ezra asks, a trace of a smile on his lips.

"Please," I repeat. His assault on my throat is evident by the streaming from my nose and eyes behind my glasses. A mess of his creation. Grabbing my hair, Ezra drags my mouth back over the length of his cock and when he's fully seated, my breast is freed from my bra. Fingers roll my nipple, pinching harshly - and it's exactly what we both needed.

Salty cum slickens the back of my throat as I groan, my core seizing. I cum for the vibrator, for the butt plug, for Lucas. And Ezra cums for me. The room fills with moans, with hands fisting desperately to see out the pleasure. My body shakes with the force of my climax, although Lucas doesn't relent on my clit. Not until I've orgasmed harder than I ever have in my life and my limbs go limp.

Ezra withdraws, leaving the taste of him in my mouth as I pant, "Now we're even."

"Ha!" Ezra shouts. My eyes are heavy as I drag them up his gorgeous body, his cock still as hard. "You thought it would be that easy? I haven't filled you with half as much cum as I intend to." I hide the rising panic, thinking he means now, but Ezra tucks himself back into his boxers and leaves the room. One by one, Lucas withdraws the objects still in me and attends to freeing my ankles and wrists. They scream in protest as I'm eased to my feet and stumble into Lucas' chest. Scooping me up, I'm carried into the adjoining bathroom.

Kyan is waiting there, a full bubble bath at the ready.

"How did she do?" he asks Lucas as if I'm not even here. The pair of them discard the scraps of underwear that are still left clinging to my body, remove my glasses and untie my hair.

"I think she'll be a perfect fit," Lucas mutters. I'm lowered into the bath as Kyan makes his way to the door. It's only when I realize Lucas intends to do the same does my arm lash out, grabbing his hand to halt him.

"That's... that's it?"

"You want more?" his brow quirks, that smirk never fading. I blush, biting on my bottom lip.

"I thought..." The right words fail me. Fuck, now I'm going to sound beyond desperate. "I thought I would have at least you," I almost whisper. It's ridiculous to be shy now. After everything I've said, the times I've ran, Lucas hasn't wavered. He hasn't given harsh words or promised punishments. He chose me against his brother's wishes. Crouching by the tub, Lucas cups my face and places a kiss on my forehead.

"Test run, remember? I can't give you everything, or you'd have no reason to stay." His emerald green eyes are twinkling as he drags himself away, rock hard in his boxer shorts. Maybe I misjudged both him and Kyan. Not Ezra though, he's a raging cock munch. Opening the door, Lucas gives me one last longing look and I remember the reason I'm here in the first place.

"Lucas," I breathe, my hooded eyes struggling to stay open. It's on the end of my tongue to ask if I deserve my meds now, but exhaustion whips me away before I get the chance.

Chapter SEVEN

I wake with a pounding headache, too many voices bouncing around my skull.

"Are you hungry? I'm famished."

"Maybe the Thorn Brothers are famished too."

"They could feast on us!"

"If only Sophia would wake the fuck up."

"Okay! Okay! I'm up," I groan, sitting upright. Holding my head, I brave a look, finding the mattress filled with characters. Human, vampire, fae and all the likes. I'm not sure how or when I maneuvered from the bath to the bed, but the morning rays blinking through velvet curtains suggest I slept all night. Another day of abstinence. This one, I can already tell, is going to be a shitshow.

Sure enough, by the time I've dragged my sore ass up, dressed and tamed my knotted hair, the boys are sitting at breakfast. Their minions, who I now recognise as the rest of the basketball team, fill the rest of the seats, not leaving one for me. Typical. Lucas gives me a shit-eating grin, pushing his chair back to pat his knee. I don't argue, slumping over to drop into his lap. Helping myself to his yogurt and rabbit food, I finish the entire bowl before he leans forward to speak.

"How are you feeling today?" he asks, soothing a hand over my ass. I tense, feeling him hardening beneath me.

"*Horny,*" Candy nudges my left arm. "*Lustful,*" Aria elbows my right. Angus appears spread horizontally across the table with a jelly worm dick in his hand.

"Do you think I could get a clozapine?" I blurt to no one in particular. "Just one would be enough for a little while." I've resorted to begging, the heel of my palm cemented against my forehead. No one responds until I force myself to look back into Lucas' green eyes. He's the ringleader, he decided I should play their little games.

"Well, I suppose it depends on if you're going to stay with us or not?" His smile flattens for once, seriousness filling his face. I shoot out of his lap, rage fueling my actions as I kick the table leg and instantly regret it.

"Why?! Have I not earned them back by now? You said if I rejected your proposal, I could return to the dorm with a full stock of pills."

"Indeed. And if you stay here, you will have to learn not to rely on them." Lucas replies coolly. My jaw drops. Characters linger on the edge of my vision, all stepping forward to crowd me. I can't breathe amongst them, the very air stolen from my vicinity. Unlike those I normally visualize, these aren't for mere distraction. These are the antagonists, evil silhouettes who wait on the sidelines for when I'm about to crack. Waiting for the chance to swoop in. To command me, control me.

Through it all, like a glowing beckon, I focus on the brightness of Lucas' eyes. My fingers twitch to reach out and steady myself on his broad shoulders, but they might as well be pinned to my sides. There's no use trusting the wobble in my legs either. The quickening rise and fall of my chest is detrimental to the tightening inside. I can't draw a full breath, yet am breathing too fast at the same time. There's not enough air, not enough time.

Vaguely, Kyan tells everyone else to leave, followed by scraping chairs and a flurry of movement. Not around me though. Those shadows cling close, sneering in my face, anticipating my downfall. My eyes are hooded again but not from exhaustion. This is much worse.

"Sophia," my name is called as if I'm underwater. Hands touch my arms, steadying me when I'm prepared to pass out. There they are again - green eyes like a lighthouse calling me home. I just wish it was that easy.

"Was I not enough for you last night?" I whimper. The question surprises even me, stemming from a place of vulnerability. Swallowing back the rising tears that accompany my words, I rephrase. "Why are you punishing me?" Fuck it, the tears come anyway. Thick streams running the lengths of my cheeks, dripping onto my band t-shirt.

"I'm not punishing you, Feisty." Lucas tugs a strand of blue hair behind my ear, the rest of his words becoming muffled. His touch is soft, loving, but the dark voices invading my mind think otherwise.

'Liar. He's using you because you're a slut. He wants you confused, easier to take advantage that way. A mindless sex doll for his brother fetish. You're only good for one thing.'

"Sophia? Did you hear what I said?" Lucas frowns, his face coming back into view as I faded out. My head drops back, strong arms catching me and the darkness seeps in for good.

***

"What do you suggest?" Lucas' voice is clipped. Even before I open my eyes, I've tuned into his mood. It's unlike him to speak so harshly, and anyone who hasn't had fitful dreams of being an unworthy whore would mistake his tone for concern.

"My advice is to give her back her prescribed medication. She was given them for a reason." The second voice is unfamiliar. I fight against my eyelids to open but the blinding lights waiting on the other side make it impossible. A metallic crash causes me to flinch, my arms seizing painfully around the needles embedded in the crooks of my elbows.

"She's not going back on that shit!" Lucas shouts, clearing the fog from my mind in an instant. I hear Kyan quietly soothing him, offering to speak with the doctor outside. Great, I'm in a freaking hospital - my least favorite place to be.

My senses quickly catch up with my mind, the scent of lemon detergent tingling my nose. From this position, fully reclined on my back, the rigidness of my denim shorts and bagginess of my t-shirt imply I haven't been stripped down and changed. That's a relief, because there are some questionable bruises and a bite mark on my body I'd rather not have to explain.

"I get what this is," Ezra speaks so suddenly, I flinch again. I hadn't realized he was also in the room. "Because your birth mom overdosed on hallucinogenic shit. You think you can be a savior this time." A weight sits on the edge of the mattress. Unfazed, Lucas takes my hand in his, stroking circles with his thumb. Ezra sighs from across the room. "You can't fix her."

"She's not broken. She's confused," Lucas' voice is small but steady.

"You want to undo years of trauma in one semester?" Ezra scoffs. My heart is batting around like a ping pong ball and I'm immensely thankful no one hooked me up to a heart monitor. "You're getting married as soon as you graduate. This isn't the time to start feeling sentimental." Wait, what? Ezra moves closer, leaning over me to get Lucas' attention. "This isn't our battle to fight. I admit, she's interesting. But she's also complex, Lucas. Just let her go and we'll pick a new pet. An easier one." *Wow.*

My gut sinks, a sickening feeling taking over. I can't disagree, but it doesn't lessen the hurt. Lucas, though, he doesn't seem to care.

"It's my turn to choose, and I chose her. The real her - not some drugged up version." I shift then, because if I didn't twist my head to the side, I'd choke on rising emotion. I knew today would be a shitshow, but this is something else. Hands cup my cheeks, the outline of Lucas giving me enough reprieve from the bright lights to peel my eyes open.

"Hey beautiful, you're awake. Scared me for a minute there." Just like that, his easy smile is back. A rasp escapes me, my throat parched. Lucas is quick to offer a cup of water, rising the recliner bed and tilting the cup against my lips. It comes as no surprise each of my movements are tracked by an array of characters in my immediate proximity.

The room is nothing like I imagined - and not a hospital after all. The clinic's private room with a lone hallway window provides a state-of-the-art bed, which Angus is sprawled across the foot of. Candy is smacking the control of the personal TV, yelling that she needs her daily dose of Judge Judy. Mania is by the water dispenser, while Aria strokes Chesh on one of the large, leather armchairs beside Ezra.

"The doctor said it was just a panic attack," his icy blue eyes roll. *Just.* I find the strength to scowl at him.

"You'll receive the best care here, I'll make sure of it." Lucas adds, regaining my attention. My heart melts for the way he's looking at me. Auburn hair flopping aside, green eyes filled with warmth. His hands are everywhere, stroking, caressing. Like he... cares.

"Your... your brothers are right," I finally manage to force past my lips. "You should pick someone... easier." A ball forms in my throat and I look away.

The whole 'pet' idea is a stupid one anyway, but after last night - I'd be lying to say I wasn't curious. They only pleasured me with toys. I bet having their bodies, their undivided attention, is an experience I'd never forget. If I weren't me. If I were normal, I'd jump in head-first. But I'm not what they intended. And then there's mention of a marriage?! How the hell does my life always find a way to become so messy?

Shifting, Lucas kicks off his sneakers and climbs into the wide bed beside me. The silkiness of his basketball attire allows him to slip beneath the sheet with ease, his shoulder dropping to indicate I should put my head there.

"Luckily for you," he sighs and I can still hear the smile in his voice, "I never do as I'm told. The exact opposite in fact." Ezra grunts in agreement. I swallow thickly, hunting for something to say when the door opens. Kyan appears, his dark eyes meeting mine in an instant.

"Hey Sport," he crosses the room on long strides and proceeds to scuff up my hair. "Back in the land of the living?"

"It's debatable," I snort, giving Candy a side glance. She's given up on the TV and is now in the hall, attacking a vending machine.

At the rate I'm going, I wouldn't be surprised if the Thorn Brothers were all part of my delusions and I'm actually locked in an institution somewhere. At least Kyan blocks my view of Ezra while his fingers linger in my blue hair a few seconds longer. As always, I can't decipher what is lurking within his fathomless dark eyes.

"What are you looking at?" I break first. Kyan half smiles.

"Your eyes," he muses. "Under these lights, they're sparkling like the bluest crystals." The air around us freezes, a rare silence settling within my head. I've always thought my eyes were my best attribute, hence why I dye my hair to match. To accentuate them so that when I look in the mirror, I don't just see the girl who fought her way into a juvenile detention center. The one who was a product of her step-father's making, and instantly regretted who she'd become when those metal bars clanked shut. I withdrew into myself the day I was locked up. But now I lay here, stripped bare by the onyx eyes consuming me. Nowhere to hide. No room to pretend.

"How about when you're ready, we get out of here and go for a swim?" Kyan cuts through our stare-off, tilting his head. I almost smile, already imagining how diving into the serene blue could wash away my worries for a while. The voices don't seem to follow me when I'm underwater. But it's the resurfacing, it's everything hitting me at once, which is the issue.

"Ugh, I can't afford to fall behind with classes any further. If I'm too late to get back, I have to study at the very least." Kyan frowns, withdrawing his hand as if I've insulted him.

"You're with us now, you don't need-"

"Of course," Lucas interrupts, inclining his head. "Studying it is. You're one of us now." I catch how Lucas corrects Kyan's words but I don't comment. Not when Lucas heaves up my bag of textbooks which was tucked beside the bed, almost as if he knew I'd say that.

Kyan doesn't object, fetching an overbed table and helping Lucas to set up my space. He's even brought his own MacBook. I merely sit there, watching the pair of them fuss until the screech of chair legs slices through the room. Ezra drags his armchair to the side of the bed, his face grave as he points to my notebook and sighs.

"Come on then. Read through to section three and take notes. I'll be quizzing you and I won't go easy."

Chapter EIGHT

It turns out, the swim was non-negotiable. We stayed at the clinic until the sun began to set, and by the time we left, I didn't have half as many worries to wash away. Ezra was true to his word, testing me vigorously and marking my answers harsher than any exam board would - but it helped. In fact, I pushed myself harder just to prove him wrong, while Lucas typed up extra notes and Kyan supplied us with endless coffee refills and vending machine snacks. After a while, I didn't even realize Candy and Angus were still watching in the background.

Floating on my back, I drift gently in the waves while the others competitively swim lengths. The four of us have the entire pool to ourselves, which I'm sure isn't a coincidence. Glass cut-outs span the domed ceiling, allowing for the starry night to leak inside. Around the edge of the dome, LED strip lights have been dimmed. The main source of light bleeds from the lavish locker rooms where our clothes, bags and the horde of my delusions are waiting.

From the edge of my peripheral vision, Kyan is climbing the ladder to the tallest diving board - again. I've decided he's the adrenaline junkie of the group, continuously throwing himself into the air with a whoop or a holler. He twists without the need to try, his flawless body rotating mid-air until his hands join into an arrow to enter the water with minimal splash.

"Show off," I mutter and smirk. Not more than a few moments later, hands drag me beneath the surface. I buck out, bubbles streaming from my mouth as I scream. My assailant manages to stay out of sight by the ink spill my darkened blue hair creates around my face. Kicking upwards, I manage to inhale a full breath before those hands are on me again. Tugging on my feet, another set of arms band around my middle. A solid erection presses against the ass of my red bikini and a third frees my breasts. They're all here, circling me like sharks. I can't fight, and in all honesty - I don't try that hard.

I'm tugged backwards, my lungs beginning to burn for air as we reach the edge of the pool and I'm allowed to surface. My feet scrape the steps until I'm drawn into Kyan's lap, his arms around my middle acting as a restraint. Ezra pops up from the water, Lucas at his side. The pair of them stride in slow motion style with rivets of water dripping down their abs. They know what they're doing. Taunting me, seducing me.

I forget all about my exposed breasts until Lucas cups one, causing me to gasp. My nipple pebbles in his hand, Ezra rolling the other sharply between his fingers. Like sugar and spice, yet again their approaches are polar opposites, yet have the same result. One which Kyan discovers when his hand dips into my bikini bottoms.

"So wet," he purred, lazily stroking circles around my center.

"Well, yeah," I reply too breathily. "We're in a swimming pool." All three of them chuckle but I don't care if they see me blush. Not when Kyan spreads his knees to open up my legs and shifts by bikini aside. Ezra sinks down onto his knees, ravaging my pussy with the expected vigor. Sucking my clit hard, he splays me wide open with deft fingers, his tongue traveling south to eat the wetness from my cunt. Like a man starved, his tongue is relentless. My mewls fill the pool room, bouncing around the dome ceiling. Ezra always seems to be punishing me, and I'm not complaining.

My eyes crack open to find Lucas watching. His all-seeing green eyes are fixated on my face, his hands still working my breasts into a frenzy. I buck against Kyan's hold, twisting my head into his shoulder. His face greets me there, a strained and desperate kiss passing between our lips. No matter how much these men, these brothers, give me - I need more. More pleasure, more connection. Kyan's tongue swirls in my mouth in a similar fashion to how Ezra's circles my channel, digging deeper than any man has before. Whatever he's searching for, I give to him within a minute of blissful torture. On a strangled cry, I clench, convulse and cum on Ezra's tongue, my body only easing when he sits back and licks his lips clean. *What are they doing to me?*

"You've been such a good girl, Feisty," Lucas comments. His fingers trail my jaw, his thumb stroking my bruised lips. "So good, in fact, I think you've earned some cock tonight." My heart stills, a shudder running the length of my body. I'm not cold, not with Kyan's heat pressing into me as solidly as his erection, but goosebumps line my arms regardless.

"I agree," Kyan adds. "Who are you going to choose, Sophia?" His purr rumbles against my ear lobe before Kyan takes it into his mouth and playfully nibbles.

"Who, err... what?" I struggle to focus. Beyond horny and dripping wet, I couldn't care less for their mind games. "Not... all?"

"Not quite," Lucas grins wider than I've seen the Cheshire cat smile. "You're not quite ready for us all yet. Choose who you'd prefer to take you this time. The others will watch." Flames ignite in my core at just the thought. I know who I want, and his cocky shit-eating grin knows it too.

"Lucas," I breathe, barely any sound coming out. Kyan doesn't hesitate, whisking me up into his arms and carrying me into the locker rooms. I catch his gaze a few times, wondering if he's pissed and if he is - he doesn't show it. Untying the bikini straps, Kyan strips me naked, strokes his fingers over my hip and heads for the wooden bench. Ezra joins him there and my eyes widen.

"Wait, you mean... here?! As in here, and now?" I ask Lucas as he casually meanders through the adjoining hallway. There's a swag to his step, a cocky attitude from being chosen first. At some point, I'll have to inform him the only reason I didn't choose Kyan was because I'm semi-scared of the piercing rumor.

"Something you should get used to rather quickly," Lucas says, reaching for my wrists. "Being our pet means we take you when we like, where we like, how we like." He pushes me a step back into the lockers, pinning my arms above my head. "Consider having the choice as a one-time courtesy. After we've fully claimed you, you're all ours."

His mouth descends on mine, igniting a heated passion between us within an instant. I wriggle free, my palms instantly pushing against his chest, but not with any conviction. I want Lucas exactly where he is, his tongue invading my mouth and senses. I love the way he tastes; smoky and spicy, even with the scent of chlorine dripping from his auburn hair. I gather all of my strength and shove him away properly this time, panting. "Your brothers are just going to sit and watch?" I swallow hard.

"It's not like they haven't seen it all before," Lucas smirks cockily.

"I know." I duck aside when he tries to grab the back of my neck, using the droplets coating my skin to my advantage. "But this is different. If you're actually, like, entering me," I blush hotter than ever before. All three of them laugh this time, loud and unfazed. Lucas reaches for my waist, pulling himself back flush against me.

"Oh, I'm going to do much more than that to you Feisty," he murmurs. "And yeah, they're going to watch it all. Take notes on how to make your chest flush, what makes you scream, how beautifully you break." My knees buckle at his words, my arms wrapping around his neck of their own accord to stop me from collapsing. At the same time, Lucas' fingers thread into my wet hair, gently easing my head back.

"Open," he says, his mouth closing over mine again. His kisses are rough, as dominating as the man before me. I'm weak for him, regardless of the fight I gave. Lucas isn't the spoiled asshole I thought. Or maybe he is, but the way my body reacts to him can't be ignored. Fingers slowly play across my shoulders, down my sides to my waist and then dip between my inner thighs, making me ache with desire.

Moments later, his fingers enter me and I cry out in ecstasy, welcoming the rush of pleasure coursing through my body. Lifting my leg to grant access, Lucas uses his free arm beneath my ass to lift me higher, caging my body against the lockers. His thrusts become harsher. Crazed. My body begins to tremble.

"Lucas," I whimper into his mouth. My kiss becomes sloppy, distracted, but Lucas naturally takes charge. He knows exactly what he's doing to me. His pace doesn't falter, his palm slamming against my clit. The friction of my back against the cool metal is breathtaking. My hands roam all over Lucas' body, feeling his muscles tense with each movement. His biceps flex, his arm pumping. My nails leave traces along his shoulder blades, his back, his neck. No patch of skin I can reach goes unmarked as I hurtle towards the blinding heat of an orgasm unlike any other.

"Do it," he encourages and I'm only too happy to obey. As if my body was waiting for permission, trying to block out the stage-fright of having two other pairs of eyes watching my every expression. Clenching around Lucas' fingers, he continues until I come back to earth. Lifting his two fingers in the air, he smirks.

"You know the drill." My eyes widen, confused who he's speaking to until Kyan appears. Dipping his head, those endless onyx eyes remain on me as he sucks on Lucas' fingers. I tremble again, a whimper trapped within my throat. Lucas chuckles against my chest, his hips helping to suspend me in the air. "Sophia likes it when we clean her juices from each other, don't you baby?"

"As long as it's not your cock," Ezra grumbles from the bench. I can't respond, and luckily, I don't have to. Kyan slinks away and as I prepare for Lucas to put me down, he tugs at his swim shorts for his dick to spring free. *Holy mother of veiny shafts.*

"Don't look so surprised. You choose me, remember?" Lucas bites his bottom lip playfully, stroking his dick along my pussy. Between my wetness and the rush of water droplets rolling down my heated skin, my body is ready for him. I moan, my head lolling to the side and giving him all the permission he needs.

Clamping his hands around my ass, Lucas drives into me in one harsh thrust. I scream out, instantly remembering myself. They're all watching, learning, and some stubborn voice in the back of my mind - probably Candy's - doesn't want me to make it easy for them. Locking my arms around his neck, I bury my face into his collar bone.

Those large hands on my ass tighten, giving Lucas enough grip as his pace increases in an attempt to dislodge me. The slapping of wet skin combines with the jingle of the lockers, but not a sound passes my lips. Not until a handful of my hair throws my head back on a pained hiss, and I could have bet who'd be there. Ezra glares at me, his blue eyes ice cold and penetrating.

"My brother told you to flush, scream and break for us. We don't like repeating an order twice." *An order*, my mind relays back. Kyan appears on Lucas' other side, the three of them shoulder to shoulder as I'm fucked, thoroughly and completely. My cunt is screaming for another release, my body trembling as Kyan's large hand slips around the base of my throat. Not squeezing, but there to deliver a message.

Regardless of who's dick is pounding inside of me, regardless of who I chose, they were all going to be my dominators tonight. All prepared to take pleasure from my suffering.

My toes curl as Lucas' mouth closes over my neck, sucking and biting. The sensation paired with the movement of our groins slapping is too intense; much more than anything I've ever experienced before. When I'm sure I'm going to pass out from the overload of sensation, someone's fingers seek out my clit and I'm lost. The combination of pleasure and pain, the stroking and the biting, is enough to make me see stars explode behind my eyes. Lucas groans in time with my own, his mouth finding my ear.

"You're so close," he whispers, his teeth scraping against my earlobe. "I can feel you shaking. Are you ready to come with me, Feisty?" My body jolts against him as if I've just been electrocuted. That's all I need to tip over the edge, taking Lucas with me. I feel him swell, but any sudden questions I had of Lucas' intentions to explode inside of me are quickly diminished. His dick is whipped from me in an instant, those same fingers from my clit replacing him. Pumping two, three long digits at the same punishing pace Lucas has set, I detonate, my teeth sinking in my bottom lip.

"Scream," Ezra barks and I obey. I call out Lucas' name again and again, as he pumps his cock and explodes all over my stomach. I barely notice, my body and legs growing numb. Tears slip from the corner of my eyes. It's all too much.

By the time I'm a jerking mess and slumping against Lucas' chest, my nails have cracked against his skin. Rivets of blood stream south.

"What a fucking mess," I sigh, too weak to care. Multiple chuckles respond, Kyan cupping my cheek.

"Welcome to life with us," he kisses my forehead. I'm passed over, cradled in Kyan's arms and walked towards the showers. It's only when Ezra lathers up his hands and proceeds to wash me down, I realize we all have a part to play here. Outside of this shower, Ezra may act as if he hates me, but I'm his pet too. He'll care for me when it really matters, I think.

Chapter NINE

"Is this seat taken?" I smile at Letty, gesturing to her side. The lecture hall isn't half filled yet, considering I'm *early*. Finally, at last, I'm awake and caffeinated enough to be early to class. Let that be an omen for the rest of today.

"Oh hey! No, not at all - come sit," Letty moves her backpack. I settle, pulling out the foldable table from between the seats and positioning it in front of me. "I haven't seen you all week, I was starting to worry." I smile easily, setting up my notepad and textbook. Everyone else present is typing on a laptop but I prefer good old fashioned paper and highlighters. It helps organize my mind. When

I don't respond, Letty tosses her brunette braid over her shoulder and presses me further. "Have you been sick?"

"Erm," my cheeks flush. How can I casually announce I've not left Thorn Manor for the past few days? Don't get me wrong, I've probably studied longer and harder than anyone in this room, between countless orgasms and several naps. I have to admit, it's been glorious, even if we're still on a one-at-time regime. Letty's large eyes blink, still waiting for my answer. "Not physically. I just needed a few mental health days, you know how it is." Her smile grows as she eases back into her seat.

"Oh absolutely - you have to look after yourself first. Not everyone is comfortable taking those days when needed so good for you. At least you're better for the sports rally this evening." I swallow thickly as the others rush down the aisles, dropping into seats as Mrs. Patrick enters the hall. She commands everyone's attention as my mind wanders. Again.

No matter how many times Candy has told me to, I've refused to ask the brothers what tonight will bring in terms of publicly claiming me. In fact, I've avoided discussing the whole 'pet' situation at all costs. If I say it, if I accept it out loud, it'll become real. It'll change the casual routine I'm settling into. Sustenance, study, sex, sleep. Complete bliss, until I need to leave the house and re-enter the real world.

Hence why I sought out Letty, figuring I'll get answers another way. I wait until Mrs. Patrick begins reading a segment of Shakespeare, letting herself get carried away, before leaning into Letty's side.

"Can I ask you something?" I whisper. Letty nods, keeping her eyes forward. "I saw the poster about the Pet-Internship. I just... I don't understand why three men like the Thorn Brothers would want to share one woman. Surely there are so many girls throwing themselves at their feet?"

"It goes back to their orphanage days," Letty replies, keeping her voice low. "From what I understand, they were constantly running away and there was a time the three would need to share a single meal or swap around who would get to wear a jacket that day. For nostalgia, I suppose, they just like to share, and this is their last chance to do so." My gut coils into a ball, my heart tugging heavily in my chest.

"What do you mean?" I look out the corner of my eye. Letty slumps lower, covering her mouth with her hand.

"I don't have all the details. Something about a prestigious family in Dubai who were seeking an arranged marriage for their daughter. They have big connections with the adoptive father and his business, so it made sense one of the Thorns would take her as his bride. Lucas is the oldest," Letty half shrugs. "He'll be wed and living in Dubai by the end of summer. Whoever they've chosen as their last pet, they'll need her to unite them more than any of the others have."

"*No pressure then*," Angus waddles across the back of the seats in front. I startle at his appearance. Since the hospital, only Candy has stuck around. She's the leech I can't withdraw from my system, the crutch I'm too dependent on. But even she hasn't been as present when I'm comatosed from cumming and drowning in dick.

"Miss Chambers," that familiar shrill voice comes. I drag my gaze from the gummy bear jumping for my attention, finding Mrs. Patrick sneering at me instead. "Would you like to indulge us in the ways Shakespeare uses environmental imagery in his work?"

"Gladly. Shakespeare used descriptions of the landscapes to convey important messages and are essential to the plot. For instance, in "A Midsummer Night's Dream," the imagery of the Moon plays a vital role in building the story and dialogs between the characters." I raise a brow, staring down Mrs. Patrick until she gets the message to leave me alone from now on.

Turns out, Ezra grilling me has its uses. We already covered this module of the course and have started on the next. If I get top marks in his next pop quiz, Ezra has promised to eat me out like a crazed lion destroying a carcass - his words. Mrs. Patrick stands stunned, before moving on to insult someone else's intelligence. It was rather ballsy of her to call me out after Kyan's warning, but I don't need his protection. I can handle myself just fine.

For the rest of the lesson, I force myself to concentrate. Despite my mind reeling, my heart both heavy and light at the same time, I won't fall behind. Won't let Mrs. Patrick have the satisfaction. Jotting down notes, managing to hold three highlighters between my fingers at once, Letty slips me a piece of paper. The address to a sorority house is written in perfect cursive, a time underneath.

"A bunch of us are getting ready for the rally together. You should join," she smiles as the bell rings. I nod shakily, tucking the paper into my back pocket. Did I just make a friend? A real one? Packing up, I praise myself until my head lifts and I spot Angus sitting on that same chair, his legs swinging.

"Enjoy it, lassy. They willna be ya friend after they discover ya secret." Twisting my mouth, I swing my backpack through his body, dislodging him from my mind. Little fucker. I just wish he wasn't right.

Chapter TEN

Clinking our glasses together, Letty and I down pomegranate mojitos before she finishes painting my face. Standing behind, Jess continues to braid my hair, giving me the full Waversea cheerleader look. Her vanity mirror has been turned away to not spoil the surprise. Giggling and music swirl around the pale pink and cream decor, several girls dancing while they change. There are easily twelve of Letty's friends in her sorority bedroom, making the huge suite seem small.

"All done," Letty smiles at her handiwork. Her brown hair is pulled tight into two chunky braids, a yellow crop top and black mini skirt exposing her athletic body. Planting my backpack in my lap, she nudges her head as if to say 'scram,' so she can start painting the next girl. I slink away, seeking out the bathroom for a moment of peace. My cheeks may be hurting from smiling, but I can't maintain being social for too long. Closing the door, I rest against it and sigh.

"*So, are you going to wear it?*" Candy's voice rings in my head before I open my eyes. She's sprawled in the bathtub, her biker boots crossed at the ankles. Casually looking at the backpack clutched in my hands, she blows a bubble of gum in the same pink as her wavy hair. I know what she's referring to.

Dropping the bag on the counter, I pick out the red ribbon box. No one was home when I retreated back to Thorn Manor after class, but this box and Angus were waiting for me on my bed.

'Last minute practice before the game. See you there, and wear this. L. x'

I peer inside for the second time. The lingerie is exquisite, unlike anything I've ever seen before. Split into three pieces, the bra, corseted middle and panties are crafted from black lace in a flower design. The shoulder straps and back of the thong are fine threads of diamonds, matching those which crisscross over the stomach.

"*Well?*" Candy prompts. I roll my eyes.

"Of course I'm going to wear it." Stripping, I pull on the underwear, cinching my waist as tight as I am able in the corset. How's this for dressing my age, mom? The lace kisses my skin, rubbing in all the right places to tantalize me all evening. Thicker rose motifs cover somewhat of my modesty, at the apex of my thighs and over my nipples.

Braving a look in the mirror, my cheeks flush. I look completely different, starting with the absence of my glasses. Letty insisted on contacts to save ruining her face paint - twin lines of swirling dots around my eyes in the team's colors. My hair has been braided on either side of my head, the top gelled up into a mohawk which floats down my back. My fingers toy with the edge of the lace against my stomach, hardly recognising my own body.

"You nearly ready, Sophia?" Letty asks through the door and I jolt.

"Yes, just coming!" I shout back, quickly grabbing the rest of my clothes from my bag. Tugging on skinny jeans, I then shrug on a yellow blouse which struggles to close around my now-pronounced cleavage. I slowly button the front, watching my secret lingerie become concealed and then stuff my feet into my white Converse. Alongside the gift box, a pair of black heels had been provided and I decided to leave them behind. No thank you blisters on my first game night. The music cuts out as I open the door and blend into the exiting crowd, following their parade of laughter all the way to the sports arena.

Posters line the sidewalk, cheering emanating from ahead. I force myself to follow, despite all instincts screaming to run away. If the crowds weren't enough to make me feel claustrophobic, the thought of this 'public claiming' has my gut tightening in knots. Is it going to be as medieval as it sounds? Perhaps it was foolish of me to avoid asking, because now the unknown is threatening to suffocate me from inside.

The path curves around the back of the building, avoiding the open field I was running through merely a few days ago. So much has changed in such a short space of time. I'm either a horny fool or a gullible idiot. Striding towards the rear parking lot, an entrance appears beyond parked coaches. Both have Radley spray painted across the sides.

The sound of drums pound through my being as I step over the threshold, my lungs seizing at the sheer amount of people present. The bleachers are packed, the crowd split into yellow and red. Homemade banners are thrust into the air, a mixture of booing and cheering making my head spin. In the center of the court, a referee and an umpire appear with microphones, their voices booming through speakers.

"Ladies and gentlemen!" the first shouts. Letty grabs my hand, tugging me towards the stairs. "Welcome to the quarter finals! Prepare yourselves to witness an exciting clash between these two talented teams. Get ready for a thrilling match filled with passion, skill, and determination." Another round of cheers is punctuated by drummers parading around the edge of the court. "Put your hands together to welcome our competitors, Rrrradleyyyy!"

Cheerleaders accompany the players leaking from the far side of the court, their jerseys black and red. Many have red stripes through their hair, and all have fists pumping in the sky as they break apart to goad the crowd. Being tugged towards a seat on the end of a row, I don't know where to look. Color and noise assault me so that none of the voices in my head can bleed through. It's only when the umpire speaks again and the crowd lessens their roars, do I hear the Cheshire cat laughing.

Large eyes and a stripy tail appear before me, spinning and twirling towards the court. Diverting to a corner I hadn't previously seen, he lays upon a gold and red throne as the Warriors are announced. And there they are, in all their glory. As if they command the light, Kyan, Lucas and Ezra shine brighter than any of the other players as they run out onto the court to a deafening cheer. And rightly so, because they're freaking gorgeous. A perfect mix of blonde, black and auburn hair, the definition of tanned muscle and chiseled jaws. Letty once described them as gods, and I can see why.

"Fuck, they are so hot," Jess looks over to fan herself. From beside me, Letty sighs.

"I'd give my left tit to be their pet. I wonder who the lucky bitch is." Keeping my gaze forward, I slink into the seat, hoping the brothers won't be able to pick me out. This was a terrible idea. What the hell was I thinking?! All I wanted was a quiet life in a new school, to leave my past and my delusions behind. Making friends would have been an added bonus, and I'm about to blow that too.

"You know what," I mutter to Letty, "I actually feel kinda sick. Might be the mojito disagreeing with me. I'm going to grab some fresh air." Letty's eyes fill with concern but she nods, letting me slink down the steps towards the exit. Using the distraction of those hollering and swaying banners around, I make it all the way to the bottom step and round the bannister. Then I feel it. The hairs rise on the back of my neck, the weight of attention searing the back of my head.

Frozen to the spot, all I manage is to look over my shoulder and see those three pairs of haunted eyes on me. Only Lucas smiles, his sneakers eating up the space between us. With his attention, comes that of the entire audience and the umpire.

"Hold up folks, we have one more announcement which needs to be made!" *No, no, no, no, god fuck no.* I make a run for it but Lucas is too fast. His hand grabs my bicep, whirling me against his chest as the other two appear to block me in.

"Where are you going, Sport?" Kyan asks at the same time Lucas speaks.

"Where's the outfit I gave you?" Shuddering, goosebumps line my skin as his green gaze tracks my cleavage. "Oh Feisty, the time for hiding is over." Hands seize me, tearing at my clothes until I'm left standing in the diamond embedded lingerie. I squirm but refuse to scream, knowing it's useless. No one would hear me over the wolf whistles, and no one would help. This is a game to them all. A cheerleader steps forward with a pair of black Jimmy Choos in her hands.

"Told you she wouldn't wear the heels," Ezra growls, accepting them and kneeling. Numbly, I allow him to remove my sneakers and guide my feet into the shoes, putting me six inches closer to Lucas' gaze. A strip of leather is threaded around my neck, tightened as the collar seals my fate, and I merely stand there.

"Why are you doing this to me?" I ask quietly, tears filling my vision. He reads my lips and frowns. Genuine hurt passes his features as the umpire announces me for the entire school to see.

"The newest, and last there will ever be, welcome the Thorn Brother's Pet!" The crowd goes crazy with a mix of cheers, boos and then there's Letty and her girls. Braving a look in their direction, they're stunned, gaping. I shy away, letting Kyan slip his arm into mine as Lucas takes the other side, Ezra up front holding the leash high for all to see. I'm led over to the throne. The court side seat where I am to remain on display in my lingerie for everyone to see. Clearly the feminist movement didn't reach this corner of the state.

My ass grazes the velvet purple cushioning, my knee crossing over the other and my back rigidly straight. There's two lessons I took from my time at juvie - show no fear. Even when you're dying inside from self-hatred or humiliation, you can't let anyone know. The second lesson is in the act of zoning out. Multiple characters instantly appear at my distress, barricading the court from sight. Even as the umpire reels off rules and a booming klaxon sounds for the game to begin, it's Chesh on my lap who has my attention.

"*Could have been worse,*" he tries to reason.

"*Dude,*" Aria scowls, planting a hand coated in fighting wraps on my knee. "*They stripped her and left her here to be gawked at. I wouldn't be surprised if people started throwing tomatoes.*"

"At least they're only mortal," Mania chimes in, blocking the view of the net which was scored in the first two minutes. *"Imagine how messy this would all be if those bitches glaring this way had mutant powers."* I don't look in the direction Mania has suggested. I can only hope Letty isn't feeling betrayed enough to sneak payback. I don't do well being backed into a corner, and a violent lashing out is on the horizon.

"Save it for those it should be directed at, honey," Candy leans on Aria's shoulders. Angus is perched upon her head, holding a mini banner which says, 'Kill the Cunts'. My nostrils flare. Candy is right. I'll save my anger, let it fester until the right moment. Drumming my fingernails on the throne arm, I sit back for Angus to entertain me with his cheerleading chants. Every other word is a curse, but watching his jiggly ass try to twerk is pretty funny.

Outside of my protective bubble, chaos reigns. My head thrums with sound, a rogue commentator nearby relaying back the game I refuse to watch. The Warriors aren't working together as well as usual, and maybe it has something to do with their key players being distracted. Radley, however, are on full form thanks to a new captain. I hear this all, yet I couldn't care less.

Instead, I drown out everyone. Those in reality, those in my mind. Before my eyes, I will the room to transform. Vines coil around the basket poles, thick with thorns and pulsing with purple roses. Bark, akin to the muesli the brothers eat every morning, ripple across the court's flooring, softening the sound of sneakers hitting the wood. From the bleachers, a canopy of trees lurches forward, distancing me from the arena but also filling it with shadows. Pockets of darkness which I use to tuck away all those in my eyeline. This is where my talent flares. Where I can wrap myself in a safe blanket and leave my troubles far behind.

Time drifts by, my numbness in my limbs barely resinating. I'm too preoccupied watching a butterfly flutter past, dancing with a squirrel hanging on a low-baring branch. The next klaxon which echoes around the arena doesn't even make me flinch, my senses dulled to my true surroundings.

"Half time," Ezra smacks my thigh and grabs the leash. "Get your ass back here." Tugging me along, my eyes are hazy, unable to catch up. I've slipped too far, false imagery lingering on the edge of my vision as I look around. Lucas and Kyan are right behind. Stumbling into the locker room, the door is slammed closed with the rest of the team outside. The quietness inside somehow hurts my ears even more than the arena, like a ringing I can't stifle. Then I remember where I am. Who I'm with. At the first opportunity, I rip the leash from Ezra's hand and tear the collar off.

"Did you all enjoy that?" I shove at his chest, kicking off my shoes. "Objectifying me?!" Another shove into the lockers. "Am I just some joke to you?!" Arms grab me from behind but I keep my glare on Ezra. He's so much easier to be angry at, because I know Lucas hasn't just upset me. He's hurt me. As if I even meant anything to him at all.

"Calm down," Kyan grunts, pinning my arms back. Red coats my vision like a raging bull is released within. Doubling my efforts, I kick Ezra in the skin, wishing I'd left my heels on.

"Why would you choose me for this bullshit? Pick any other whore with no self respect. I never wanted this. Now the entire school has seen me in my underwear, sitting on the sidelines like a court jester." My nostrils flare as I'm dragged backwards and forced to sit in Kyan's lap on the bench.

"That's not…," Lucas appears, running a hand through his auburn hair. "It wasn't like that."

"Oh really? Please enlighten me - what was it like?" There it is again - that same hurt from earlier. I hate it when he doesn't smile, but it's not my job to placate him.

"You have a throne in our direct eye line. We wanted to show you off," Lucas mumbles, his hands raised in defeat. I'm not buying it.

"As your slutty pet," I spit. Ezra darts forward, gripping my chin and tugging my face upwards.

"As our Queen, you idiot. Having you there bolsters us, makes us feel special to have the most exquisite woman in the room as close to the court as possible and her attention is *supposed* to be on us." I stop struggling, the air knocked from my lungs. In my peripheral vision, all of the female characters who plague me are shaking their heads, and had those words come from the others, I may have been able to convince myself they were lying. But Ezra? Ezra hasn't said one sweet thing to me. I doubt he'd start now if it weren't true.

"We didn't mean to ridicule you," Kyan adds softly beside my ear. "We only want to..."

"To?" I push when no one continues.

"Worship you," Lucas answers, kneeling before me. "The second we graduate, I'm being shipped off to be married. I don't get to date, to feel butterflies, to enjoy the cat and mouse flirtation game. This is the extent of my relationships."

He toys with the diamond straps at my shoulders as Kyan's hold on my arms loosens. Ezra's blue eyes soften for the first time, his hand resting on Lucas' shoulder. This is what they live for. The three of them, brothers of pure survival, who will do whatever it takes to remain bonded. Including dating together, screwing together.

"That's what this has all been about," I breathe as understanding dawns. Lucas nods and even Ezra joins him on the floor.

"I wanted to feel as connected to my brothers as possible until I leave, and to have fun. The pet thing was a simple solution. Girls usually jump at the chance and... I'll admit, it got kinda out of hand. No one has ever fought against us before. No one has been like you," he brushes a hand over my cheek. "You're unique, special. You make us work harder and the reward is so much sweeter. I'm so glad you're the one we get to have this last experience with."

I have no fight left. He should have told me, but again - would I have believed him? That the rich kid who could have anything, anyone in the world, wanted me? Leaning forward, my forehead connects with Lucas', a sigh filling my chest.

At this moment, he reminds me of a billionaire I once read about. One who's twisted friends plotted and participated in his sex life for the good of their friendship. And as I pull back, a new addition to my delusional line-up has appeared.

"*You're the main character of this story, Sophia,*" Amethyst winks at me. Her purple hair flows over a black PVC catsuit. "*Show these boys why you needed to be their last. There's no replacing you.*" I smile in her direction, pushing up to my feet. Retrieving the collar and heels, I re-dress myself how they wanted me.

"Come on then, you guys have a game to win." I offer the leash to Ezra. It's as much of a peace-offering as he'll get. When I surrender myself to the three of them later, they'll know the truth. I'm ready to commit to them fully for the upcoming semester.

The three of them are banded around me when we stride back towards the court. I don't hear the boos this time. I tune out everything except for the gentle strokes against my arms and thighs. Let people stare, let them be disgusted.

As degrading as this seems, as twisted and fucked up, I can do this for Lucas. For the sacrifice he's making for his family, I can give him this. Hell, I'll do more than that. I'll embrace it and make sure I also have fun along the way. At least for the next several weeks. I am their Queen after all.

Chapter ELEVEN

"Allow me," Kyan offers his hand. I smile, stepping down from the throne which has been mounted in the back of a pick up truck. After the Waversea Warriors took the win, I was paraded back to Thorn Manor with my champions around my feet. Even I have to admit, it was exhilarating waving to the cheering crowds who followed, whilst multiple hands stroked my calves. Amongst all of these people, I'm still their focus.

Attempting to hop down from the truck, Ezra swoops in to toss me over his shoulder, ass in the air. The cheers grow louder, accompanying us all the way to the front door until they're slammed outside. Planting me down on the heels, Ezra crowds me against the nearest wall, his body radiating heat through the dark. He prefers it this way, I decide. Concealed within shadow, anonymous outlines who rely on touch and base instinct. I feel his breath on my neck as he leans down, his lips dangerously close to mine. The cheers of the crowd have faded away, and all I can hear is my own ragged breath and the beat of my heart.

Reaching up to my face, his fingers trail my jawline, stopping at my chin. I'm trapped, caught in his all-consuming presence, unable to break away. Ezra, the man I've yet to truly connect with. The one I offered myself in the library and he rejected. There's no denying the electricity between us now, the tension building until it's almost unbearable.

"Just fucking kiss her already or I will," Lucas comments from somewhere within the adjoining room. On a muffled groan, Ezra's lips crash down on mine and I'm lost. Lost to the feeling of his mouth, lost in the sensation from the rough claim of his tongue. I wrap my arms around his neck, pulling him closer, inviting him in deeper. Ezra's hands down my body, pulling my hips into his. I gasp as he grinds his solid length against me, those silk sports shorts doing nothing to conceal his arousal. It works to stir my own higher, and suddenly - I want him.

I want Ezra to take me right here, rewrite everything I thought I knew about myself and piece me back together. My fingers tangle in his blond hair, pulling him into me encouragingly. His heart pounds against my own, his hands sliding up my stomach to my breasts. I arch into his touch, my body begging for more.

"Warm her up for us Ez," Kyan slaps him hard on the back, breaking our trance. "We need to shower."

"What he means is," I turn Ezra's face back to me, refusing to let our moment be ruined. Not when we've waited this long for it. "Make me come at least twice before they get back."

"*That's my girl*," Candy mutters in the background. I feel her drifting away from me, withdrawing into a tiny box in my brain where she and the others belong.

I'm quickly distracted from that thought, as Ezra picks me up and walks me through the house. Between strides, his lips seek out mine over and over. Unable to resist the insatiable taste of danger. Each touch tells me he wants everything I've got to give and more. No words are said. None are needed. We're both one with the moment, our bodies begging for more.

My back is lowered onto a mattress. As he continues his exploration of my lingerie, I release a quiet moan, the sound swallowed by his mouth. Coming to rest his warm palms on my hips, he lowers himself over me, the hard line of his erection against my stomach.

Pushing the shorts past his erection, I grab his length and stroke him in my palm. Ezra lets out a muffled sound, his tongue flicking against my neck. Coiling his fingers against the thin lace between my thighs, he tugs it aside to find me soaking from anticipation. The pad of his thumb is instantly in place, barely moving as he circles my clit. I shudder beneath his touch, reeling for more. He stops, a rare smile gracing his face as he denies me.

"Please Ezra," I whimper, wanting to feel him in other places. I squirm in the hopes for added friction. "Give me more."

"Not a chance," he slowly shakes his head. "You're so fucking hot like this." Eyes hooded, chest panting, I shake my head.

"Fine, have it your way." Rolling out from under him, Ezra doesn't try to stop me. I stand and walk over to the chair, similar to one I have in the corner of my room, preparing to give Ezra a strip show, starting with my corset. His arms move to settle beneath his head as my finger delicately pop the clasps at the back. One by one, until the threaded diamonds are dismantled and the middle scrap of lace falls away. I hook my fingers into the sides of my thong, rolling my hips in time with the music in my head. Slowly pushing them down my thighs, I can't help but stare at the man reclined on the bed.

He's a mixture of the asshole I thought I knew and the Dom I've come to understand - someone who can control my body with a flick of his wrist, a lick of his tongue. His icy blue eyes are hungry, his teeth sinking into his bottom lip.

The door handle turns, becoming stuck and a round of banging pounds on the other side of the wood.

"The fuck, Ez? Open up!" Lucas shouts and my mouth drops open. He's locked us inside.

"Please, continue," Ezra tilts his head. His begging sounds so similar to my own just a moment ago, and it's my turn to smirk.

"Not a chance," I echo back. "You look so fucking hot like this - with blue balls, I mean." Striding for the door, I pop the lock before Ezra manages to catch me, his arms banding around my middle. Lucas bursts inside, Kyan right behind with towels bunched at their waists. A fight takes place, my feet swept from the floor as Ezra jumps up on the bed and uses me as a barricade. The others join a second later, their towels forgotten and cocks half-mast. A glint of silver catches my eyes from Kyan's particular region.

"She's mine!" Ezra shouts, taking me by surprise. Lucas lunges first, trying to pry me free while Kyan attacks Ezra from behind. Biceps bunch around my head until suddenly, we're freefalling onto the mattress. Laughter spills, limbs tangle. Amongst the damp skin and wandering hands, a mouth finds mine. The atmosphere turns heated in an instant, no more stalling as my breasts are pried free from the bra and my thighs are widened.

Clouding my vision, Lucas' green eyes remain on mine, his tongue swirling around my mouth. In the background, I vaguely hear the vibrations before my clit is blessed with the pulsing rhythm of a wand. I arch and groan, Lucas not giving me a moment's reprieve. This is how they like me, lost to the passion and unaware of what they plan on doing next. Delving into the kiss, the heated chase of tongues, nibbling teeth and bruising lips, Ezra makes a strangled sound from between my legs.

"Focus on me baby. I was instructed to give at least two orgasms before the real fun begins." He doesn't play around either, ramping up the vibrations and lazily pushing his fingers inside of me, twisting and tugging down. He doesn't have to wait for my first one, the anticipation is too much to bear. For the second, Ezra replaces the wand with his tongue and his fingers trail further back. Toying with my ass, I tense, suddenly remembering this is it. The night I take all three and I'm not sure I'm ready.

"Relax," Kyan murmurs beside my ear. It's him teasing my nipples, pinching to the point of pain and then rubbing the aching pebbles across his palm. Lucas senses the change in my body, releasing me from our kiss to prop himself beside me.

"You're ready," Lucas reassures, stroking along my jawline to the base of my throat.

"And if you're not, we'll stop," Kyan adds. Ezra, his face buried in my pussy, mutters something incoherent which I can only imagine is a - 'no, we fucking won't.' I should be assured, but my thighs tighten, risking cutting off Ezra's air supply. All three of them, at once, inside of me. Chewing on my bottom lip, Kyan pries it free.

"What are you scared of, baby?"

"Your... um, your piercing," I whisper, flames heating my cheeks. If Ezra wasn't pinning me down, I'd probably run away and lock myself in a closet somewhere. Kyan chuckles, shifting to kneel beside me. And there it is, or rather - they are. On the underside of his shaft, a solid metal bar through the gland beneath his plump purple head has two small balls either side.

"This is the frenum," he shows me, nudging the bar with his thumb. This cock is a thing of beauty, silky smooth and free of any foreskin. His hand travels south. "And this is the lorum," Kyan strokes the horizontal bar at the base of his shaft and top of his balls. "Nothing to be scared of. Here, let me show you."

Reaching for my head, Lucas lifts my upper back and nudges himself underneath, propping me up as Kyan guides his dick into my mouth. The cold metal of his piercing touches my tongue, aided by the salty musk of arousal radiating from his shaft. We've only just begun, yet he's ready to have me, to take me in any capacity I'm prepared to give. His length is hard against my lips, yet he moves slowly and carefully, allowing me time to adjust. As I take him further in, I feel the metal bar hit the back of my throat as the second one slides across my tongue. Not painful or as intrusive as I imagined. A gentle stroke, an added sensation I can only imagine will drive me crazy inside my pussy. I groan, his cock vibrating within my throat.

"Not so bad, right?" Kyan asks. I don't answer, Ezra commanding my attention once more. Sucking my clit hard, a finger sinks into my ass. A moment of pain and blind panic are quickly chased away by the pleasure he brings. Instead of retracting, Ezra's finger spins, rotates, teases. I tremble, my body no longer my own.

With Lucas's focus on removing my bra and toying with my nipples, the sensation of having three men pleasing me at the same time is overwhelming. Kyan's piercing rubs against my tongue as I move my head up and down, growing bolder, exploring the different textures and sensations that can be created from his body. Ezra's experienced fingers work their magic between my legs with a combination of expert teasing and gentle caresses, making me moan uncontrollably in pleasure. Every inch of Kyan fills my mouth as he begins thrusting deeper and deeper, enticed by the humming. I am so lost in the moment that nothing else matters but pleasure. Mine, theirs, ours. My commitment to being their pet drives me even wilder.

My orgasm rips through me so intensely, my scream is stifled by dick. Kyan's breathing becomes more labored as I suck hard, riding through the intensity as if my life depends on it. Waves of coursing pleasure take over my body, causing me to jerk and flinch uncontrollably. Lucas holds me in place, Ezra not relenting until I go slack. Then I fall back on Lucas, the remaining trembles leaving a blissful tingle through my entire body.

"That makes two," Ezra kneels upright. If I thought they'd give me a moment to catch my breath, I couldn't have been more wrong. I'm flipped, dragged and repositioned over Lucas' cock. I know the drill by now, I am to suck the monstrosity before me until I can't breathe whilst trying to contain myself from giving in to these boys too easily. These men, adverse in sexual torture and advocates of my darkest fantasies. Making himself comfortable against the headboard, Lucas shifts his legs horizontally, giving Kyan room to slide beneath me. Ezra is at the rear, standing at the foot of the bed and stroking my ass.

"Do you still hate us, Sophia?" Kyan asks, toying with my nipples. I groan.

"So, so much," I lie, still too conscious of appearing weak. Too aware I'm one in a long list of Pets. I want to be different. I want to make *them* work for it, force them to remember me.

"Good." Ezra spanks me so harshly, I cry out and ruin my unaffected facade. "Hate-fucks are so much better." I hear the bottle of lube being opened, but it's Kyan who has my attention.

Gently holding my hips, he lifts and lowers me over his jutting cock. His touch is electric, sending shivers down my spine as I surrender to his offered embrace. Arms band around my back, his muscles creating a cage of comfort while his dick slides into me. I'm wet enough, even without Ezra's lubed fingers circling and sliding into my ass. Those piercings add a heady sensation, my cunt so completely filled, I'm sure there's no room for Ezra as he lines up with my ass. Again, so, so wrong.

Ezra makes room, driving me further into Kyan's hold. I bite down on his collar bone, withholding a scream. It's too much, too intense. Pain twinges with a burning that makes my eyes water, but once fully seethed, Ezra stills. It's up to Kyan to roll his hips, sending all three of us into a frenzy. Strained groans fill the room, the most incredible feeling uniting and twisting through the three of us. We're caught in the euphoria of the moment, lost in each other's passion, but there's someone missing.

Kyan reads my mind, gripping my ribs to stretch me further up the bed. My nipple slips into his mouth with ease, and Lucas watches the scene like his favorite porno. Stroking his cock, his green eyes consume me. I'd happily tumble into this realm of Wonderlust if I could keep his obsessive gaze on me. Licking my lips, with two cocks filling me, I eagerly take Lucas into my mouth. All three at once. Candy would be so proud. There's no time for delusions now, my mind too distracted by the silky shaft easing into the back of my throat as if it was molded to fit.

"Tell us how it feels to be ours," Lucas demands, driving into my mouth harder. His words take me as much by surprise as the intrusion.

I clench my teeth together, stilling his thrusts whilst refusing myself from falling any harder. They can have my body, make me more vulnerable than any other, but my mind is my own. Realizing I wouldn't answer, even if he withdrew his cock and allowed me to do so, Lucas smirks.

"Fair enough, I'll go first. You're insatiable. The perfect fit, the perfect choice. No one has suited us all this well before. Right, Ez?"

"Damn fucking right," Ezra says on a pained grunt. Not physically pained, but the type of blissful torture one feels when tethering on the edge. I know because I'm right there with him.

"So fucking perfect," Kyan agrees. Moving on to my other nipple, his expert hands massage my breasts and slip down towards my clit. I quickly slap him away. I can't handle any more, not when his steady pace is hurtling me towards a climax which will shatter us all.

My heart picks up a beat. Kyan's hot breath fans my neck. With every kiss he places against my collar bone, I float higher. Drift further from my body when I'm no longer overwhelmed by the fullness but at one with it. With them. Kyan's hips roll in a perfect rhythm to the bobbing of my head. Lucas moans softly. Ezra holds firm, his cock a dull weight pushing against all the right places. All moving together in perfect harmony.

The stirrings of my orgasm increase. Intensify. Their expert fingers explore every inch of my body - cupping my breasts before moving downwards to stroke my clit in tantalizing circles. As I slip into a state of pure ecstasy, our collective energy builds around us. Every muscle in my body is ready to explode, my hips arching as the pleasure reaches its crescendo.

We all realize it at once - our coming together. Our moment to solidify this connection. My skin crackles with electricity as hard bodies press against mine and, with a final sharp thrust from Kyan, I suck

Lucas hard. So hard, my cheeks hollow out as the first wave of pleasure courses through me.

Stars flare behind my eyes. I'm hit with an orgasm that knocks the air from my lungs with its force. Ezra growls, cumming inside of my ass. The pulsing of his cock spurs on my own screams. Still pumping warm cum, he slowly withdraws, the release as pleasurable as the entry. I tilt my hips back, calling a mixture of their names when I'm flipped on my back.

Kyan's weight presses down onto my chest, my legs held wide at the ankles by Lucas and Ezra. Increasing his pace, Kyan fucks me. So hard, so deep, I'm certain he's pounding directly into my soul. My orgasm triples, drawn out with the ferocious slamming of his cock. I'm soaking, screaming and spent by the time Kyan whips out, coming into a discarded towel.

Just as I moan, fighting to catch my breath, a warm tongue licks my pussy. Strokes my clit. Looking down, I find both Lucas and Ezra cleaning me of my own cum, multiple hands pinning down my thighs. I buck regardless, rasping for words. When they fail, I reach out and run my fingers through their hair.

"You taste so good, Feisty." Lucas smirks at me, green eyes twinkling. "Do you like having two men lick your pussy?"

"Yes." I bite my lip as my cheeks flame red.

"Good girl." Ezra grins. Sighing and content, I rest back, savoring the hot strokes they provide. A soft caress. A loving brush. Conformation they care for me. I've been waiting for this.

We remain there for what feels like an eternity, until finally our blissful moment fades and reality slowly creeps back in. I'm panting, dots peppering my vision. Shifting, I expect the three men to move around me, changing positions like a carousel. Rotating to give each a turn - but that's not what happens. Instead, I'm eased up the mattress, cocooned in by the hard planes of their bodies. They've barely broken a sweat, so the break is for my benefit. I don't question it, not as I instinctually snuggle into Kyan's side, my limbs heavy as my voice.

"Lucas?" I breathe. "You were never going to give me back my meds, were you?" Of all the times to ask such a question, this is most likely the worst. But I don't want to fall asleep beside them with it playing on my mind. Cupping my cheek, Lucas gently twists my head backwards to see the serenity in his gaze.

"No, Feisty. I was never going to let you dull your true self. From the moment you propositioned Ezra in the library, I wanted you as mine. Not some drugged up version, but the version of yourself you were scared to let the world see."

Tears well in my eyes, spilling over as I close my lids. Lucas presses a kiss to one side, Kyan kissing away the other. Ezra has settled himself between my legs, his head on my thigh. He's not as open as the others, not as able to express himself, but I understand. In small glimpses, Ezra has shown me he wants affection, but like me, he struggles to accept it. Hiding behind a mask is far easier. Turns out the Thorn Brothers were as desperate for acceptance as I was.

Tiredness drags me into a soft lull, my breathing becoming deep. Yet, there's a smile on my face. I'm officially their pet now. Publicly claimed, fully initiated. The last one who will connect them before life tears them apart. We all have our role to play here, and as I lie in a cage of their protection, I vow not to take my meds again. Even if they were offered, I'd find another solution. Lucas believes in me, and it's time I believed in myself. The Thorn's Pet is perfect, chosen, revered. It may not be forever, but for now - it's exactly what I need.

Epilogue

One Year Later...

"So basically, the raven who has been following her for eight years turns out to be a shifter, who also happens to be her pledged guardian and her fated mate." I rush out in one excited breath, my eyes wide and cheeks flushed. Gripping the bound pages in my hands, I thrust it towards the panel in front of me. "Until a small group from the Vampire army arrives to take her to their territory, since she is the exiled princess of two rival species."

"I can see you enjoyed it," my boss at the publishing house chuckles. Enjoyed it? I devoured the manuscript in less than twelve hours. Pretty much since I left work last night with it tucked beneath my arm, until

I needed to have a triple espresso to be able to stagger back into the office today. And it was worth every second.

"I highly recommend we publish everything this author touches. She has a way of combining angst, lust, multiple love interests, intricate plots and twists into everything she writes. We'd be fools to pass up such an opportunity."

"Your advice and enthusiasm are duly noted, Sophia. Let me talk figures with my team and I'll let you be the one to put in the call to..." he flicks through his notes for the author's name.

"Maddison Cole, two D's," I supply, my smile wide enough to hurt. That's a call I can't wait to make, but the shadow on the other side of the glass door beckons me to step away for now. Thanking the panel for indulging me forty-five minutes longer than intended, I step out into the hallway, practically vibrating with excitement.

"Well, how did it go?" a female asks. Once upon a time, it would have been the female character from my latest read - in this case, Aspen, but those days are over. I turn and throw myself into Letty's arms.

"Amazingly! They're going to sign the author to us. You know what that means," I wiggle the manuscript. "I get first look at all of her works from now on!"

"Okay well, as happy as I am for you - it's well past lunchtime and it's Taco Tuesday. Only a true friend would wait around this long for you to finish blabbing out the entire storyline of the book she's pitching."

"I didn't blab the whooooole story, I didn't say anything about the gut-wrenching, heartbreaking twist where-"

"Yeah, yeah. You can talk at the side of my face while I eat," Letty rolls her eyes. Sliding her arm into mine, she drags me down the hallway and into the opulent elevator. This past year has been a whirlwind of hard work and lucky breaks. After graduation, I was hired on the spot at my first interview, and the following Monday, I was sitting in a booth beside Letty. We've managed to rise through the ranks together, growing closer day by day until we officially became roommates. Now, both sitting pretty as editorial directors, we have certain freedoms. One including longer lunch breaks and all at the company's expense.

Her stomach is growling as we rush through the main lobby, glass reflecting across the marbled flooring. The sunlight isn't deceiving, as we tumble into the busy street and sigh at the warmth of summer. We fly to Europe next week, touring Italy from Venice to Rome and everywhere in between. I can't wait, and the best part - I don't have to declare all of my medication each time I fly anymore.

The Thorn Brothers did many things to my body, for my mind, but the one I'll always hold dear is boosting my self-worth. I haven't touched an antipsychotic since arriving at Waversea, swapping my remedy of choice to therapy instead. Along with Dr. Ramsey, we've delved deep into my need to surround myself with imaginary characters. They were a defense mechanism, and like fight-or-flight, the height of my unease triggered them.

Now, I only see Candy when I want to. To tell me an outfit looks good or if I should have another shot. She keeps me on the precariously thin line between good and devilishly naughty. I haven't had any other characters assault me since - not from books at least. Lucas, Ezra and Kyan... they often bleed from my dreams into everyday life, just to remind me how amazing our twelve weeks together were.

"Earth to Sophia, I was talking to you about Italy," Letty snaps her fingers before my eyes. I blink rapidly, realizing we're at the restaurant next door already. A cute, small establishment which is always heaving. Waving to the owner behind the bar, the middle-aged jolly man chastises us for being late.

"Blame it on me," I smile sweetly, navigating the occupied seats to our reserved table in the back. Thanks to the weather, the sliding doors have been pulled back, only a small fence dividing our seats from the street outside. "Okay, talk to me - I'm ready," I nod, laying a cloth napkin over my lap to protect the expensive pantsuit.

"So packing," Letty continues, "I was thinking to only take little summer dresses and interchangeable sandals. Easy access for the Italian lovers I'm going to find," she winks. It's my turn to roll my eyes.

"As long as you don't bring them back to the hostel. We're sharing a bunk bed." A basket of breadsticks is placed between us, one automatically finding its way to my hand. Chewing absentmindedly, I start off thinking about how many books on the 'to-be-read' list I'll be able to get through on my eReader whilst away, but soon divert to thinking about this apparent heat wave. I wonder if Lucas will be affected by it too. I wonder a lot of things about Lucas, mainly if he's okay.

I've purposely avoided searching him up online, knowing his wedding would have made the news. Ezra and Kyan too, no doubt, have gone on to take the world by storm. Championship basketball players, dating A-list celebrities, attending all the latest premieres and award ceremonies. Luxurious lives for lavish men, and I'm happy for them. Truly. What we had, all four of us, was incredible. Beyond my wildest delusions, and memories I will alway treasure.

But life goes on. I meant something to them once, but not anymore. I have no claim to Lucas, and without him - it wouldn't feel right with the others. No, I promised myself not to dwell, only appreciate.

"Oh for fuck's sake," Letty groans. "Will you stop drooling all over that breadstick? Is my voice really so bland that you zone out everytime I speak?" I chuckle, Letty's words reminding me of Mrs. Patrick. I spent the second half of the semester imagining her as a squawking dodo after Ezra rushed me through the coursework with weeks to spare.

"Take it as a compliment, your voice is just too melodic." Sharing a smile, a waitress brings us two mojitos on the house. We shouldn't really drink whilst on our lunch break, but Letty and I are already in full vacation mode. It's only Tuesday, yet we've finished all of our tasks way ahead of schedule. Those which need revising later in the week, we've delegated to interns.

"Do you miss them?" Letty asks, catching me off guard as I sip my drink. I don't need to ask who she means - the three men I *never* speak of out loud. Although I'm certain she hears me moaning their names in my sleep through the walls of our apartment.

"Of course I do. I know it's stupid-" I sigh.

"It's not stupid at all." Letty's brown gaze holds a rare seriousness. "I saw them with the other Pets. They were different with you." I know this. Even without ever seeing the brothers glance at anyone else, I could feel how in tune they were with me. Like our hearts all beat to the same drum; it was easy, it was natural. We studied together at the dining table, worked out together in the private gym, made endless love on any available surface. And even when our time was coming close to an end, there was no bitterness. Only understanding.

"Remember how you almost missed your finals?" Letty chuckles and I groan.

"Oh, don't even. I only made it thanks to Lucas causing a distraction at the door so I could stand on Kyan's shoulders and jump through the window!"

"Where was Ezra?"

"Sporting the black eye I gave him after he finally found the handcuff key and released me from the bedframe," I smirk. I'm sure he did it on purpose, losing faith in his own tutoring. He had nothing to worry about - his constant grillings meant I passed with flying colors.

"Makes for a good story though," Letty tilts her head and raises her glass.

"I'll drink to that," I agree. Downing my drink, the cocktail glass has yet to touch back to the table when Letty's eyes widen just over my shoulder. Probably some hot guy on the street has her all flustered, her cheeks turning pink.

"Hey Feisty," a deep rumble sounds. I brush my ear with my shoulder, shaking out the imaginary voice. Jeez, what was in that drink? "Long time no see." Letty's mouth is open now and my brow furrows. Wait - that's not a delusion. Standing in a rush, I spin and come face to face with an overly tanned version of Lucas. A crisp black suit hugs his muscled frame, those biceps appearing to strain against the jacket. His auburn hair is a flash of vibrant red, his green eyes beaming down at me. My mouth turns dry, no words forming.

"Sorry it took so long. I had some… legal affairs I needed to straighten out." My gaze leaves his easy smirk, and travels down to the hands clasped in front of him. No wedding ring in sight.

"You," my voice is too breathy, "you didn't get married?"

"It wasn't fair on anyone to lie. My heart belongs elsewhere, and I'm here to claim it back." I don't breathe. Don't dare move in case this perfect scenario shatters and I suddenly wake up. But then, it gets even better.

"We all are." Kyan steps into my eyeline, all shaggy black hair and endless onyx eyes. In direct contrast with his blond curls and icy blues, Ezra appears from Lucas' other side, completing the trio. *My trio.*

"You mean, all of you and me? You all want just me?" I echo back like a parrot. My mind reels to catch up. One semester was the plan.

An encapsulated amount of time we all agreed on. But this? Now? My eyes remain on Ezra, his acceptance the one I need to hear the most.

"Get in the fucking car, Sophia," Ezra growls, jerking his head to the Bentley pulled up behind. "We're taking you home." Through his scowl, a small smile breaks free and my heart flutters. I vault over the mini fence without a second thought, diving into their arms. Any and all arms who will have me. Lips touch my forehead before I'm tugged across the sidewalk. I call back for Letty to tell work I've gone home sick for the rest of the day. Probably the week.

"Bitch, don't forget about Italy!" she hollers, waving a breadstick at me. Dropping into the back seat and closing the door, I lean through the open window but it's Lucas who responds from the driver's seat.

"We've upgraded your trip. A limo will pick you up next week to bring you to the private jet. Hope you don't mind a couple of tagalongs." Kyan, beside me in the back, angles himself across my thighs.

"And about those Italian lovers," he shouts for everyone nearby to hear. "No need to hold back. You've got your own penthouse suite to fill." My mouth drops open as the blackout window starts to rise. Before it reaches the top and shuts me away from the outside world, Letty's whooping slips through.

"Your boyfriends are the best!"

"Yeah, they really fucking are," I agree, catching all three sets of hungry eyes on me. My teeth sink into my bottom lip, the atmosphere tripling with lust and I already know - this vehicle isn't going anywhere until I'm wrought with pleasure and three orgasms deep.

"*That's my girl,*" Candy winks from the passenger seat, propping heart-shaped sunglasses over her eyes and waving goodbye as she fades away for the last time.

Afterword

Yeah, I know. You need a stiff drink and several orgasms. Go for it – I'll wait.

Jesus, you still going? Wow, impressive stamina. Get back to it.

Feeling better now? Great.

I hope you've enjoyed reading Sophia's and the Thorn Brother's story as much as I got carried away writing it! These characters will live rent-free in my mind for a long time to come! As mentioned in my confession, this story was a taster of my writing style. I've tried extremely hard to pack the same amount of angst, attraction, smut and emotion into such a short space, as you'd usually find by me. Thank you for reading, whether for the first or the fiftieth time! Your support fuels my fire and keeps me writing in my darkest days.

So I'm guessing the question is, what do you do with your life now? Well, I've got you fully covered in all holes – I mean, on all fronts! Without even realising it, because I am a wordage wizard, you've already been introduced to a huge variety of characters from my backlist. On the following pages, you'll discover further background of each of our leading ladies and the books they feature in. Have fun and reach out to me soon – I love hearing from and talking to readers <3

Introducing Candy

Have you ever wondered what Harley Quinn would have been like as a biker? Armed with her baseball bat and Angus, her imaginary best friend who also happens to be an angry Scottish gummy bear, Candy is about to show you! When the Gambling Monarchs steal her last job from the mafia and leave her for dead, this biker gang is in for a shock. They should have known this gum-chewing, unapologetic badass doesn't hold grudges - she squashes them.

The Books in this Completed Dark Comedy RH Series:

- Findin' Candy (prequel novella)

- Crushin' Candy – Book One

- Smashin' Candy – Book Two

- Friggin' Candy – Book Three

Blurb for Book One:

S'up? I'm Candy. Excuse the name. Mom was a stripper back in her prime and I was a client gone wrong. Now stuck behind the bar, she was eager for me to join the family business. *No thanks.*

The only circles I run in are the ones my bubblegum bubbles make. Don't worry about my teeth though, sugar-free as always. I'm not a complete psycho. Oh, except for my passive-aggressive, potty-mouthed, imaginary best friend who happens to be a gummy bear. That part is pretty nuts.

I was thoroughly enjoying myself, doing whatever the hell I wanted until a group of model-worthy bikers try to muscle in on my heist. They don't seem to realise those with barely any personal belongings tend to grow protective of what's theirs, and by taking one of my beloved possessions, they've signed their own death warrants. Fooling them with a sickly sweet smile, I'll slip past their defences and claim back what's rightfully mine, no matter the cost. Putting bullies back in their place when no one else can is my speciality. No one screws over Candy Crystal twice.

P.S, yeah - stripper name game is on point.

Introducing
Amethyst

Today...she's Amethyst, tomorrow...who knows? Being a con woman sure has it's perks, and dwindling spoiled billionaires is all part of the fun. Until Amethyst stumbles in Myles Hudson's limo. As the master of disguises, Amethyst must rely on her wits to survive the reformed sex addict and his three best friends. However, there's no bracing her for the strict and unhealthy routine Myles is trapped in. Suddenly, her target isn't to steal from Myles, but to save him from those who claim to have his best interests at heart.

Books in this Billionaire RH series (so far):

- Wreckin' Amethyst

- Unravelin' Amethyst (pre-order)

- Treasurin' Amethyst (To come Spring 2024)

Blurb for Book One:

Money doesn't buy happiness. Payback does.

A con artist by trade, Amethyst is used to hiding in plain sight. She's a master of survival, adopting any character necessary to find the answers she seeks.

Caught in the act robbing a jewellery store, Amethyst finds herself at the mercy of four drool-worthy billionaires. Thrust into a world of business deals and bribery, she must discover what agendas these seemingly respectable men hold, and how they plan to exploit her with them.

Can Amethyst expose the secrets alluding her? Or will fighting the attraction Amethyst harbors for her captives be the biggest con she has yet to pull?

A Night of PLEASURE and WRATH

Introducing Aria
(in Harlow's story)

Raised in care with her to foster brothers, Aria is used to fighting. An MMA fighter by day, crime enthusiast by night, her life seems complete – until she meets Harlow. Innocent naive Harlow, who needs to learn a thing or two about underground fighting if she is to survive. Unfortunately for Aria, those pesky brothers of hers have similar ideas about breaking Harlow and as we all know, men always think with their dicks.

The Standalone book for this MMA Fighter RH story:

- A Night of Pleasure and Wrath

Blurb:

One night. Three strangers. A newfound resentment I can't shake.

They say bad things happen in threes. For me, however, the fourth

came in the form of Club Rapture. Locked in until morning, I'm

forced to face unknown truths about myself, especially the lengths I'm

willing to go to for praise.

The Bloodied Skulls took everything that night. Stripped me bare and

left me to pick up the pieces. Abandoned. Humiliated. Thrown into

the shadows where my anger festered.

Since then on, I seek to find them and reap my revenge. They taught

me to find pleasure in my pain, yet a bitter taste of anguish is all I'm

left with. Until their blood coats my hands and they beg for my mercy,

I won't stop. This time, I'll be in control, and they'll be the ones eager

to submit.

Introducing Mania

Orphaned, as an infant, mania is no stranger to being alone. Only family is the adopted. The Demon mother awaiting her in hell, but manias ability for resurrection has her trapped roaming earth. Until that begrudged freedom is cut short. Bringing a spirit back from hell, the answers to sending him back lie within the mutant asylum-after life. As do his two brothers...

Books in this Completed Paranormal RH Series:

- Queen of Crazy – Book One

- Kings of Madness – Book Two

- The Untold Story of Hoax (2.5 Novella)

- Reign of Chaos – Book Three

Blurb for Book One:

Deprived beings with genetic mutations make the best Psychos.

Pfft, f£(&*@g humans. Whoever thought genetic testing was a good idea is lucky my ability isn't to travel back in time, because I'd have pinpointed the moment he primed the first needle and strangled the life out of him. Instead I'm stuck here, hated by humans and hunted by the authorities. Mutes have no place in this world, which is why I've tried to leave it countless times, not that I could be so lucky. My destiny is to be trapped amongst the living and that's not the worst part.

Thrown into the Afterlife Asylum, I find myself falling for an actual ghost, hated by a Mutant called Ghost and bound to a fiery soul I've never met - that's my reality. These three men have barrelled into my life and destroyed the mantra I once lived by. No love means no grief, and my knack for rising from the dead means I'd be grieving for a very long time.

One day I'll figure out how to take my rightful place in Hell, where the fires are warm and the demons inviting. With the burnt ashes of sinners filling my senses and their blood-curdling screams bringing a smile to my lips. I know where I belong. Now I need to find out how to stay there, permanently.

Wonderlust

**Introducing
Malice and Chesh**

The Cheshire Cat has seen many peculiar, unexplainable things during his time, but none as strange as Malice. Crash landing back in Wonderlust twenty years after the original story, Malice is free from her human imprisonment and the antipsychotic meds she's been forced to take. If only the land she once knew is as eager to receive her. With the most of the men missing, Lust as the new currency and nothing quite as it seems, Malice truly doesn't know where she belongs anymore. The only one who can aid her is Hatter, but as he is missing, that responsibility lies with the muscular stubborn, Tweedle Boys. Did I also mention they're vampires now? Jabbercocky help us all.

Books in this Retelling Menage Duet:

- Descend into Madness

- Embrace the Mayhem (pre-order)

Blurb for Book One:

Fact: Malice is clinically insane.
Another fact: She's also completely sound of mind.

Incarcerated to a mental institution for killing her father, Malice finds peace in tea parties with dolls and talking to the walls. But the shadows of her past aren't done with her yet. A midnight break-in, a valiant rescue and a pair of twins with more muscle and fang than she remembers.

Thrown into a realm of lust and wonder, Malice quickly realises something is missing. Someone is missing. A race against prophecies ensues, the clutches of enemies tightening their grip. One twin proves an aid, the other a hindrance. If only it was clear which one was which. The stopwatch is ticking. Will Malice find what she's looking for, before a cruel twist of fate finds her?

BOUND BY FATE

Introducing Aspen

Aspen was born to be fierce. Half vampire, half werewolf, and subsequently the exiled princess of both species – no one would accept any less. Not in the least, the three vampire guards sent to retrieve her from her banishment. If only the raven who's been secretly protecting her for the past eight years would allow it. Shifting into a stunning yet secretive guardian, Aspen's cramped exile hut just became a lot more crowded – and she's definitely not complaining.

The Standalone book in this Paranormal RH series so far:

- Moon Bound

- More interlinking standalones to come in 2024

Blurb:

Exiled for existing.

Suffering is second nature.

As the rejected offspring of two rival species, Aspen has never found a place to belong. Until a trio of dark and dangerous vampires appear unannounced to relocate her indefinitely. With the object of her heart left behind, Aspen must choose between a mentor she's always known, and the new beings she can't help but crave.

Pushing her to embrace both monsters lurking within, will Aspen survive the tests that threaten to destroy her and walk away with her heart intact? Or will she permit herself to acknowledge each of those inner monsters might just have mates of their own...

Introducing
Harper

Being the new girl at a fancy college is daunting for anyone, but not for Harper. Being deaf, she's used to the challenges others don't know how to face – and she quickly adds Rhys Waversea to that equation. The school bully and righteous asshole enjoys playing with fresh meat, but the head jock isn't about to let Harper become another notch on his sworn enemy's bedpost. Clayton is troubled, quiet, protective. Even when he has no right to be.

The Books in this Completed High School Bully Menage Series:

- Perfectly Powerless – Book One

- Handsomely Heartless – Book Two

- Beautifully Boundless – Book Three

Blurb for Book One:

There's a darkness at Waversea College.

A shadow lingering behind every wall. A poisonous undercurrent, filled with malicious intent. All emanating from him.

Rhys Waversea.

Fuelled by his father's bank account and adrift in an endless boredom, Rhys would watch us all burn alive for his own amusement. Until Harper steps foot on campus.

Captivating us both with her quick wit and smart mouth, I make it my mission to keep her from harm and mostly, from him.

As tensions grow, it quickly becomes apparent the hatred between Rhys and I has only just begun.

About the Author

Writer of Dark Comedy Why Choose Romance.

Maddison is a married mum of two, and a serial daydreamer. As a huge fan of all romance tropes herself, it was time to pen the stories which consume her mind most hours of the day.

As a child, Maddison was a jet setter and has lived all over the world, only to return to the south east of England, where she is now happily settled. With a double award in applied arts and art history, Maddison is a creative with a dark passion for feisty females and spicy stories.

Join my Newsletter or on my website:

www.authormaddisoncole.com

Facebook – **Author Maddison Cole**

www.facebook.com/Maddison.cole.314

Facebook readers group - **Cole's Reading Moles**

www.facebook.com/groups/colesreadingmoles

Instagram and TikTok - **@authormaddisoncole**